The Lonesome Trail and Other Stories

by

B. M. BOWER

Other Works
by
B.M Bower

Cabin Fever
Casey Ryan
Chip, of the Flying U
Cow-Country
The Flying U Ranch
The Flying U's Last Stand
Good Indian
The Gringos
The Happy Family
The Heritage of the Sioux
Her Prairie Knight
Jean of the Lazy A
Lonesome Land
The Lonesome Trail and Other Stories
The Long Shadow
The Lookout Man
The Lure of the Dim Trails
The Phantom Herd
The Quirt
The Range Dwellers
Rowdy of the Cross L
Skyrider
Starr, of the Desert
The Thunder Bird
The Trail of the White Mule
The Uphill Climb

THE LONESOME TRAIL
PART ONE

A man is very much like a horse. Once thoroughly frightened by something he meets on the road, he will invariably shy at the same place afterwards, until a wisely firm master leads him perforce to the spot and proves beyond all doubt that the danger is of his own imagining; after which he will throw up his head and deny that he ever was afraid—and be quite amusingly sincere in the denial.

It is true of every man with high-keyed nature, a decent opinion of himself and a healthy pride of power. It was true of Will Davidson, of the Flying U—commonly known among his associates, particularly the Happy Family, as "Weary." As to the cause of his shying at a certain object, that happened long ago. Many miles east of the Bear Paws, in the town where Weary had minced painfully along the streets on pink, protesting, bare soles before the frost was half out of the ground; had yelled himself hoarse and run himself lame in the redoubtable base-ball nine which was to make that town some day famous—the nine where they often played with seven "men" because the other two had to "bug" potatoes or do some other menial task and where the umpire frequently engaged in throwing lumps of dried mud at refractory players,—there had lived a Girl.

She might have lived there a century and Weary been none the worse, had he not acquired the unfortunate habit of growing up. Even then he might have escaped injury had he not persisted in growing up and up, a straight six-feet-two of lovable good looks, with the sunniest of tempers and blue eyes that reflected the warm sweetness of that nature, and a smile to tell what the eyes left unsaid.

Such being the tempting length of him, the Girl saw that he was worth an effort; she took to smoking the chimney of her bedroom lamp, heating curling irons, wearing her best hat and best ribbons on a weekday, and insisting upon crowding number four-and-a-half feet into number three-and-a-half shoes and managing to look as if she were perfectly comfortable. When a girl does all those things, and when she has a good complexion and hair vividly red and long, heavy-lidded blue eyes that have a fashion of looking side-long at a man, it were well for that man to travel—if he would keep the lightness of his heart and the sunny look in his eyes and his smile.

Weary traveled, but the trouble was that he did not go soon enough. When he did go, his eyes were somber instead of sunny, and he smiled not at all. And in his heart he carried a deep-rooted impulse to shy always at women—and so came to resemble a horse.

He shied at long, blue eyes and turned his own uncompromisingly away. He never would dance with a woman who had red hair, except in quadrilles where he could not help himself; and then his hand-clasp was brief and perfunctory when it came to "Grand right-and-left." If commanded to "Balance-*swing*" the red-haired woman was swung airily by the finger-tips—; which was not the way in which Weary swung the others.

And then came the schoolma'am. The schoolma'am's hair was the darkest brown and had a shine to it where the light struck at the proper angle, and her eyes were large and came near being round, and they were a velvety brown and also had a shine in them.

Still Weary shied consistently and systematically.

At the leap-year ball, given on New Year's night, when the ladies were invited to "choose your pardners for the hull dance, regardless of who brought yuh," the schoolma'am had forsaken Joe Meeker, with whose parents she boarded, and had deliberately chosen Weary. The Happy Family had, with one accord, grinned at him in a way that promised many things and, up to the coming of the Fourth of July, every promise had been conscientiously fulfilled. They brought him many friendly messages from the schoolma'am, to which he returned unfriendly answers. When he accused them openly of trying to "load" him; they were shocked and grieved. They told him the schoolma'am said she felt drawn to him—he looked so like her darling brother who had spilled his precious blood on San Juan Hill. Cal Emmett was exceedingly proud of this invention, since it seemed to "go down" with Weary better than most of the lies they told.

It was the coming of the Fourth and the celebration of that day which provoked further effort to tease Weary. "Who are *you* going to take, Weary?" Cal Emmett lowered his left eyelid very gently, for the benefit of the others, and drew a match sharply along the wall just over his head.

"Myself," answered Weary sweetly, though it was becoming a sore subject.

"You're sure going in bum company, then," retorted Cal.

"Who's going to pilot the schoolma'am?" blurted Happy Jack, who was never consciously ambiguous.

"You can search me," said Weary, in a you-make-me-tired tone. "She sure isn't going with Yours Truly."

"Ain't she asked yuh yet?" fleered Cal. "That's funny. She told me the other day she was going to take advantage of woman's privilege, this year, and choose her own escort for the dance. Then she asked me if I knew whether you were spoke for, and when I told her yuh wasn't, she wanted to know if I'd bring a note over. But I was in a dickens of a hurry, and couldn't wait for it; anyhow, I was headed the other way."

"Not toward Len Adams, were you?" asked Weary sympathetically.

"Aw, she'll give you an invite, all right," Happy Jack declared. "Little Willie ain't going to be forgot, yuh can gamble on that. He's too much like Darling Brother—"

At this point, Happy Jack ducked precipitately and a flapping, four-buckled overshoe, a relic of the winter gone, hurtled past his head and landed with considerable force upon the unsuspecting stomach of Cal, stretched luxuriously upon his bunk. Cal doubled like a threatened caterpillar and groaned, and Weary, feeling that justice had not been defeated even though he had aimed at another culprit, grinned complacently.

"What horse are you going to take?" asked Chip, to turn the subject.

"Glory. I'm thinking of putting him up against Bert Rogers' Flopper. Bert's getting altogether too nifty over that cayuse of his. He needs to be walked away from, once; Glory's the little horse that can learn 'em things about running, if—"

"Yeah—*if*!" This from Cal, who had recovered speech. "Have yuh got a written guarantee from Glory, that he'll run?"

"Aw," croaked Happy Jack, "if he runs at all, it'll likely be backwards—if it ain't a dancing-bear stunt on his hind feet. You can gamble it'll be what yuh don't expect and ain't got any money on; that there's Glory, from the ground up."

"Oh, I don't know," Weary drawled placidly. "I'm not setting him before the public as a twin to Mary's little lamb, but I'm willing to risk him. He's a good little horse— when he feels that way—and he can run. And darn him, he's *got* to run!"

Shorty quit snoring and rolled over. "Betche ten dollars, two to one, he won't run," he said, digging his fists into his eyes like a baby.

Weary, dead game, took him up, though he knew what desperate chances he was taking.

"Betche five dollars, even up, he runs backwards," grinned Happy Jack, and Weary accepted that wager also.

The rest of the afternoon was filled with Glory—so to speak—and much coin was hazarded upon his doing every unseemly thing that a horse can possibly do at a race, except the one thing which he did do; which goes to prove that Glory was not an ordinary cayuse, and that he had a reputation to maintain. To the day of his death, it may be said, he maintained it.

Dry Lake was nothing if not patriotic. Every legal holiday was observed in true Dry Lake manner, to the tune of violins and the swish-swish of slippered feet upon a more-or-less polished floor. The Glorious Fourth, however, was celebrated with more elaborate amusements. On that day men met, organized and played a matched game of ball with much shouting and great gusto, and with an umpire who aimed to please.

After that they arranged their horseraces over the bar of the saloon, and rode, ran or walked to the quarter-mile stretch of level trail beyond the stockyards to witness the running; when they would hurry back to settle their bets over the bar where they had drunk to the preliminaries.

Bert Rogers came early, riding Flopper. Men hurried from the saloon to gather round the horse that held the record of beating a "real race-horse" the summer before. They felt his legs sagely and wondered that anyone should seem anxious to question his ability to beat anything in the country in a straightaway quarter-mile dash.

When the Flying U boys clattered into town in a bunch, they were greeted enthusiastically; for old Jim Whitmore's "Happy Family" was liked to a man. The enthusiasm did not extend to Glory, however. He was eyed askance by those who knew him or who had heard of his exploits. If the Happy Family had not backed him loyally to a man, he would not have had a dollar risked upon him; and this not because he could not run.

Glory was an alien, one of a carload of horses shipped in from Arizona the summer before. He was a bright sorrel, with the silvery mane and tan and white feet which one so seldom sees—a beauty, none could deny. His temper was not so beautiful.

Sometimes for days he was lamblike in his obedience, touching in his muzzling affection till Weary was lulled into unwatchful love for the horse. Then things would happen. Once, Weary walked with a cane for two weeks. Another time he walked ten miles in the rain. Once he did not walk at all, but sat on a rock and smoked cigarettes till his tobacco sack ran empty, waiting for Glory to quit sulking, flat on his side, and get up and carry him home.

Any man but Weary would have ruined the horse with harshness, but Weary was really proud of his deviltry and would laugh till the tears came while he told of some new and undreamed bit of cussedness in his pet.

On this day, Glory was behaving beautifully. True, he had nearly squeezed the life out of Weary that morning when he went to saddle him in the stall, and he had afterwards snatched Cal Emmet's hat off with his teeth, and had dropped it to the ground and had stood upon it; but on the whole, the Happy Family regarded those trifles as a good sign.

When Bert Rogers and Weary ambled away down the dusty trail to the starting point, accompanied by most of the Flying U boys and two or three from Bert's outfit, the crowd in the grand-stand (which was the top rail of the stockyard fence) hushed expectantly.

When a pistol cracked, far down the road, and a faint yell came shrilling through the quiet sunshine, they craned necks till their muscles ached. Like a summer sand-storm they came, and behind them clattered their friends, the dust concealing horse and rider alike. Whooping encouraging words at random, they waited till a black nose shot out from the rushing cloud. That was Flopper. Beside it a white streak, a flying, silvery mane—Glory was running! Happy Jack gave a raucous yell.

Lifting reluctantly, the dust gave hazy glimpses of a long, black body hugging jealously close to earth, its rider lying low upon the straining neck—that was Flopper and Bert. Close beside, a sheeny glimmer of red, a tossing fringe of white, a leaning, wiry, exultant form above—that was Glory and Weary.

There were groans as well as shouting when the whirlwind had swept past and on down the hill toward town, and the reason thereof was plain. Glory had won by a good length of him.

Bert Rogers said something savage and set his weight upon the bit till Flopper, snorting and disgusted—for a horse knows when he is beaten—took shorter leaps, stiffened his front legs and stopped, digging furrows with his feet.

Glory sailed on down the trail, scattering Mrs. Jenson's chickens and jumping clean over a lumbering, protesting sow. "Come on—he's going to set up the drinks!" yelled someone, and the crowd leaped from the fence and followed.

But Glory did not stop. He whipped around the saloon, whirled past the blacksmith shop and was headed for the mouth of the lane before anyone understood. Then Chip, suddenly grasping the situation, dug deep with his spurs and yelled.

"He's broken the bit—it's a runaway!"

Thus began the second race, a free-for-all dash up the lane. At the very start they knew it was hopeless to attempt overtaking that red streak, but they galloped a mile for good manners' sake; Cal then pulled up.

"No use," he said. "Glory's headed for home and we ain't got the papers to stop him. He can't hurt Weary—and the dance opens up at six, and I've got a girl in town."

"Same here," grinned Bert. "It's after four, now."

Chip, who at that time hadn't a girl—and didn't want one—let Silver out for another long gallop, seeing it was Weary. Then he, too, gave up the chase and turned back.

Glory settled to a long lope and kept steadily on, gleefully rattling the broken bit which dangled beneath his jaws. Weary, helpless and amused and triumphant because the race was his, sat unconcernedly in the saddle and laid imaginary bets with himself on the outcome. Without doubt, Glory was headed for home. Weary figured that, barring accidents, he could catch up Blazes, in the little pasture, and ride back to Dry Lake by the time the dance was in full swing—for the dancing before dark would be desultory and without much spirit.

But the gate into the big field was closed and tied securely with a rope. Glory comprehended the fact with one roll of his knowing eyes, turned away to the left and took the trail which wound like a snake into the foothills. Clinging warily to the level where choice was given him, trotting where the way was rough, mile after mile he covered till even Weary's patience showed signs of weakening.

Just then Glory turned, where a wire gate lay flat upon the ground, crossed a pebbly creek and galloped stiffly up to the very steps of a squat, vine-covered ranch-house where, like the Discontented Pendulum in the fable, he suddenly stopped.

"Damn you, Glory—I could kill yuh for this!" gritted Weary, and slid reluctantly from the saddle. For while the place seemed deserted, it was not. There was a girl.

She lay in a hammock; sprawled would come nearer describing her position. She had some magazines scattered around upon the porch, and her hair hung down to the floor in a thick, dark braid. She was dressed in a dark skirt and what, to Weary's untrained, masculine eyes, looked like a pink gunny sack. In reality it was a kimono. She appeared to be asleep.

Weary saw a chance of leading Glory quietly to the corral before she woke. There he could borrow a bridle and ride back whence he came, and he could explain about the bridle to Joe Meeker in town. Joe was always good about lending things, anyway. He gathered the fragments of the bit in one hand and clucked under his breath, in an agony lest his spurs should jingle.

Glory turned upon him his beautiful, brown eyes, reproachfully questioning.

Weary pulled steadily. Glory stretched neck and nose obediently, but as to feet, they were down to stay. Weary glanced anxiously toward the hammock and perspired, then stood back and whispered language it would be a sin to repeat. Glory, listening with unruffled calm, stood perfectly still, like a red statue in the sunshine.

The face of the girl was hidden under one round, loose-sleeved arm. She did not move. A faint breeze, freshening in spasmodic puffs, seized upon the hammock, and set it swaying gently.

"Oh, damn you, Glory!" whispered Weary through his teeth. But Glory, accustomed to being damned since he was a yearling, displayed absolutely no interest. Indeed, he seemed inclined to doze there in the sun.

Taking his hat—his best hat—from his head, he belabored Glory viciously over the jaws with it; silently except for the soft thud and slap of felt on flesh. And the mood of him was as near murder as Weary could come. Glory had been belabored with worse things than hats during his eventful career; he laid back his ears, shut his eyes tight and took it meekly.

There came a gasping gurgle from the hammock, and Weary's hand stopped in mid-air. The girl's head was burrowed in a pillow and her slippers tapped the floor while she laughed and laughed.

Weary delivered a parting whack, put on his hat and looked at her uncertainly; grinned sheepishly when the humor of the thing came to him slowly, and finally sat down upon the porch steps and laughed with her.

"Oh, gee! It was too funny," gasped the girl, sitting up and wiping her eyes.

Weary gasped also, though it was a small matter—a common little word of three letters. In all the messages sent him by the schoolma'am, it was the precise, school-grammar wording of them which had irritated him most and impressed him insensibly with the belief that she was too prim to be quite human. The Happy Family had felt all along that they were artists in that line, and they knew that the precise sentences ever carried conviction of their truth. Weary mopped his perspiring face upon a white silk handkerchief and meditated wonderingly.

"You aren't a train-robber or a horsethief, or—anything, are you?" she asked him presently. "You seemed quite upset at seeing the place wasn't deserted; but I'm sure, if you are a robber running away from a sheriff, I'd never dream of stopping you. Please don't mind me; just make yourself at home."

Weary turned his head and looked straight up at her. "I'm afraid I'll have to disappoint yuh, Miss Satterly," he said blandly. "I'm just an ordinary human, and my name is Davidson—better known as Weary. You don't appear to remember me. We've met before."

She eyed him attentively. "Perhaps we have—it you say so. I'm wretched about remembering strange names and faces. Was it at a dance? I meet so many fellows at dances—" She waved a brown little hand and smiled deprecatingly.

"Yes," said Weary laconically, still looking into her face. "It was."

She stared down at him, her brows puckered. "I know, now. It was at the Saint Patrick's dance in Dry Lake! How silly of me to forget."

Weary turned his gaze to the hill beyond the creek, and fanned his hot face with his hat. "It was not. It wasn't at that dance, at all." Funny she didn't remember him! He suspected her of trying to fool him, now that he was actually in her presence, and he refused absolutely to be fooled.

He could see that she threw out her hand helplessly.

"Well, I may as well 'fess up. I don't remember you at all. It's horrid of me, when you rode up in that lovely, unconventional way. But you see, at dances one doesn't think of the men as individuals; they're just good or bad partners. It resolves itself, you see, into a question of feet. If I should dance with you again,—*did* I dance with you?"

Weary shot a quick, eloquent glance in her direction. He did not say anything.

Miss Satterly blushed. "I was going to say, if I danced with you again

I should no doubt remember you perfectly."

Weary was betrayed into a smile. "If I could dance in these boots, I'd take off my spurs and try and identify myself. But I guess I'll have to ask yuh to take my word for it that we're acquainted."

"Oh, I will. I meant to, all along. Why aren't you in town, celebrating? I thought I was the only unpatriotic person in the country."

"I just came from town," Weary told her, choosing, his words carefully while yet striving to be truthful. No man likes confessing to a woman that he has been run away with. "I—er—broke my bridle-bit, back a few miles" (it was fifteen, if it were a rod) "and so I rode in here to get one of Joe's. I didn't want to bother anybody, but Glory seemed to think this was where the trail ended."

Miss Satterly laughed again. "It certainly was funny—you trying to get him away, and being so still about it. I *heard* you whispering swear-words, and I wanted to scream! I just couldn't keep still any longer. Is he balky?"

"I don't know what he is—now," said Weary plaintively. "He was, at that time. He's generally what happens to be the most dev—mean under the circumstances."

"Well, maybe he'll consent to being led to the stable; he looks as if he had a most unmerciful master!" (Weary, being perfectly innocent, blushed guiltily) "But I'll forgive you riding him like that, and make for you a pitcher of lemonade and give you some cake while he rests. You certainly must not ride back with him so tired."

Fresh lemonade sounded tempting, after that ride. And being lectured was not at all what he had expected from the schoolma'am—and who can fathom the mind of a man? Weary gave her one complex glance, laid his hand upon the bridle and discovered that Glory, having done what mischief he could, was disposed to be very meek. At the corral gate Weary looked back.

"At dances," he mused aloud, "one doesn't consider men as individuals—it's merely a question of feet. She took me for a train robber; and I danced with her about forty times, that night, and took her over to supper and we whacked up on our chicken salad because there was only one dish for the two of us—oh, mamma!"

He pulled off the saddle with a preoccupied air and rubbed Glory down mechanically. After that he went over and sat down on the oats' box and smoked two cigarettes while he pondered many things.

He stood up and thoughtfully surveyed himself, brushed sundry bright sorrel hairs from his coat sleeves, stooped and tried to pinch creases into the knees of his trousers, which showed symptoms of "bagging." He took off his hat and polished it with his sleeve he had just brushed so carefully, pinched four big dimples in the crown, turned it around three times for critical inspection, placed it upon his head at a studiously unstudied angle, felt anxiously at his neck-gear and slapped Glory affectionately upon the rump—and came near getting kicked into eternity. Then he swung off up the path, softly whistling "In the good, old summer-time." An old hen, hovering her chicks in the shade of the hay-rack, eyed him distrustfully and cried "kr-*r-r-r*" in a shocked tone that sent her chickens burrowing deeper under her feathers.

Miss Satterly had changed her pink kimono for a white shirt-waist and had fluffed her hair into a smooth coil on the top of her head. Weary thought she looked very nice. She could make excellent lemonade, he discovered, and she proved herself altogether different from what the messages she sent him had led him to expect. Weary wondered, until he became too interested to think about it.

Presently, without quite knowing how it came about, he was telling her all about the race. Miss Satterly helped him reckon his winnings—which was not easy to do, since he had been offered all sorts of odds and had accepted them all with a recklessness that was appalling. While her dark head was bent above the piece of paper, and her pencil was setting down figures with precise little jabs, he watched her. He quite forgot the messages he had received from her through the medium of the Happy Family, and he quite forgot that women could hurt a man.

"Mr. Davidson," she announced severely, when the figures had all been dabbed upon the paper, "You ought to have lost. It would be a lesson to you. I haven't quite figured all your winnings, these six-to-ones and ten-to-ones and—and all that, take time to unravel. But you, yourself, stood to lose just three hundred and sixty-five dollars. Gee! but you cowboys are reckless."

There was more that she said, but Weary did not mind. He had discovered that he liked to look at the schoolma'am. After that, nothing else was of much importance. He began to wish he might prolong his opportunity for looking.

"Say," he said suddenly, "Come on and let's go to the dance."

The schoolma'am bit at her pencil and looked at him. "It's late—"

"Oh, there's time enough," urged Weary.

"Maybe—but—"

"Do yuh think we aren't well enough acquainted?"

"Well we're not exactly old friends," she laughed.

"We're going to be, so it's all the same," Weary surprised himself by declaring with much emphasis. "You'd go, wouldn't you, if I was—well, say your brother?"

Miss Satterly rested her chin in her palms and regarded him measuringly. "I don't know. I never had one—except three or four that I—er—adopted, at one time or another. I suppose one could go, though—with a brother."

Weary made a rapid, mental note for the benefit of the Happy Family—and particularly Cal Emmett. "Darling Brother" was a myth, then; he ought to have known it, all along. And if that were a myth, so probably were all those messages and things that he had hated. She didn't care anything about him—and suddenly that struck him unpleasantly, instead of being a relief, as it consistently should have been.

"I wish you'd adopt me, just for to-night, and go;" he said, and his eyes backed the wish. "You see," he added artfully, "it's a sin to waste all that good music—a real, honest-to-God stringed orchestra from Great Falls, and—"

"Meekers have taken both rigs," objected she, weakly.

"I noticed a side saddle hanging in the stable," he wheedled, "and I'll gamble I can rustle something to put it on. I—"

"I should think you'd gambled enough for one day," she quelled. "But that chunky little gray in the pasture is the horse I always ride. I expect," she sighed, "my new dancing dress would be a sight to behold when I got there—and it won't wash. But what does a mere man care—"

"Wrap it up in something, and I'll carry it for yuh," Weary advised eagerly. "You can change at the hotel. It's dead easy." He picked up his hat from the floor, rose and stood looking anxiously down at her. "About how soon," he insinuated, "can you be ready?"

The schoolma'am looked up at him irresolutely, drew a long breath and then laughed. "Oh, ten minutes will do," she surrendered. "I shall put my new dress in a box, and go just as I am. Do you *always* get your own way, Mr. Davidson?"

"Always," he lied convincingly over his shoulder, and jumped off the porch without bothering to use the steps. She was waiting when he led the little gray up to the house, and she came down the steps with a large, flat, pasteboard box in her arms.

"Don't get off," she commanded. "I can mount alone—and you'll have to carry the box. It's going to be awkward, but you *would* have me go."

Weary took the box and prudently remained in the saddle. Glory, having the man he did for master, was unused to the flutter of women's skirts so close, and rolled his eyes till the whites showed all round. Moreover, he was not satisfied with that big, white thing in Weary's arms.

He stood quite still, however, until the schoolma'am was settled to her liking in the saddle, and had tucked her skirt down over the toe of her right foot. He watched the proceeding with much interest—as did Weary—and then walked sedately from the yard, through the pebbly creek and up the slope beyond. He heard Weary give a sigh of relief at his docility, and straightway thrust his nose between his white front feet, and proceeded to carry out certain little plans of his own. Weary, taken by surprise and encumbered by the box, could not argue the point; he could only, in range parlance, "hang and rattle."

"Oh," cried Miss Satterly, "if he's going to act like that, give me the box."

Weary would like to have done so, but already he was half way to the gate, and his coat was standing straight out behind to prove the speed of his flight. He could not even look back. He just hung tight to the box and rode.

The little gray was no racer, but his wind was good; and with urging he kept the fleeing Glory in sight for a mile or so. Then, horse and rider were briefly silhouetted against the sunset as they topped a distant hill, and after that the schoolma'am rode by faith.

At the gate which led into the big Flying U field she overtook them. Glory, placid as a sheep, was nibbling a frayed end of the rope which held the gate shut, and Weary, the big box balanced in front of him across the saddle, was smoking a cigarette.

"Well," greeted Miss Satterly breathlessly, and rather tartly, "only for you having my dress, I'd have gone straight back home. Do brothers always act like this?"

"Search me," said Weary, shaking his head. "Anyway, yuh better talk to Glory about it. He appears to be running this show. When I rode out to your place, I didn't have any bit in his mouth at all. Coming back, I've got one of Joe Meeker's teething rings, that wouldn't hold a pet turkey. But we're going to the dance, Miss Satterly. Don't you worry none about that."

Miss Satterly laughed and rode ahead of them. "I'm going," she announced firmly. "It's leap year, and I think I can rustle a partner if you decide to sit and look through that gate all night."

"You'll need your pretty dress. Glory ain't much used to escorting young ladies, but he's a gentleman; we're coming, all right."

It was strange, perhaps, that Glory should miss the chance of proving his master a liar, but he nevertheless ambled decorously to Dry Lake and did nothing more unseemly than nipping occasionally at the neck of the little gray.

That is how Weary learned that large, brown eyes do not look sidelong at a man after the manner of long, heavy-lidded blue ones; and that, also, is how he came to throw up his head and deny to himself and his world that he ever was shy of women.

PART TWO

Weary rode stealthily around the corner of the little, frame school-house and was not disappointed. The schoolma'am was sitting unconventionally upon the doorstep, her shoulder turned to him and her face turned to the trail by which a man naturally would be supposed to approach the place. Her hair was shining darkly in the sun and the shorter locks were blowing about her face in a downright tantalizing fashion; they made a man want to brush them back and kiss the spot they were caressing so wantonly. She was humming a tune softly to herself. Weary caught the words, sung absently, under her breath:

"Didn't make no blunder—yuh couldn't confuse him.
A perfect wonder, yuh had to choose him!"

The schoolma'am was addicted to coon songs of the period.

She seemed to be very busy about something and Weary, craning his neck to see over her shoulder, wondered what. Also, he wished he knew what she was thinking about, and he hoped her thoughts were not remote from himself. Just then Glory showed unmistakable and malicious intentions of sneezing, and Weary, catching a glimpse of something in Miss Satterly's hand, hastened to make his presence known.

"I hope yuh aren't limbering up that weapon of destruction on my account, Schoolma'am," he observed mildly.

The schoolma'am jumped and slid something out of sight under her ruffled, white apron. "Weary Davidson, how long have you been standing there? I believe you'd come straight down from the sky or straight up from the ground, if you could manage it. You seem capable of doing everything except coming by the trail like a sensible man." This with severity.

Weary swung a long leg over Glory's back and came lightly to earth, immediately taking possession of the vacant half of doorstep. The schoolma'am obligingly drew skirts aside to make room for him—an inconsistent movement not at all in harmony with her eyebrows, which were disapproving.

"Yuh don't like ordinary men. Yuh said so, once when I said I was just a plain, ordinary man. I've sworn off being ordinary since yuh gave me that tip," he said cheerfully. "Let's have a look at that cannon you're hiding under your apron. Where did yuh resurrect it? Out of some old Indian grave?

"Mamma! It won't go off sudden and unexpected, will it? What kind uh shells—oh, mamma!" He pushed his hat back off his forehead with a gesture not left behind with his boyhood, held the object the length of his long arm away and regarded it gravely.

It was an old, old "bull-dog" revolver, freckled with rust until it bore a strong resemblance to certain noses which Miss Satterly looked down upon daily. The cylinder was plugged with rolls of drab cotton cloth, supposedly in imitation of real bullets. It was obviously during the plugging process that Miss Satterly had been interrupted, for a drab string hung limply from one hole. On the whole,

25

the thing did not look particularly formidable, and Weary's lips twitched.

"A tramp stopped here the other day, and—I was frightened a little," she was explaining, pink-cheeked. "So aunt Meeker found this up in the loft and she thought it would do to—to bluff with."

Weary aimed carefully at a venturesome and highly inquisitive gopher and pulled, with some effort, the rusted trigger. The gopher stood upon his hind feet and chipped derisively.

"You see, it just insults him. Yuh could'nt scare a blind man with it— Look here! If yuh go pouting up your lips like that again, something's going to happen 'em. There's a limit to what a man can stand."

Miss Satterly hastily drew her mouth into a thin, untempting, red streak, for she had not seen Weary Davidson, on an average, twice a week for the last four months for nothing. He was not the man to bluff.

"Of course," she said resentfully, "you can make fun of it—but all the same, it's better than nothing. It answers the purpose."

Weary turned his head till he could look straight into her eyes—a thing he seemed rather fond of doing, lately.

"What purpose? It sure isn't ornamental; it's a little the hardest looker I ever saw in the shape of a gun. And it won't scare anything. If you want a gun, why, take one that can make good. You can have mine; just watch what a different effect it has."

He reached backward and drew a shining thing from his pocket, flipped it downward—and the effect was unmistakably different. The gopher leaped and rolled backward and then lay still, and Miss Satterly gave a little, startled scream and jumped quite off the doorstep.

"Don't yuh see? You couldn't raise any such a dust with yours. If yuh pack a gun, you always want to pack one that's ready and willing to do business on short notice. I'll let yuh have this, if you're sure it's safe with yuh. I'd hate to have you shooting yourself accidental."

Weary raised innocent eyes to her face and polished the gun caressingly with his handkerchief. "Try it once," he urged.

The schoolma'am was fond of boasting that she never screamed at anything. She had screamed just now, over a foolish little thing, and it goes without saying she was angry with the cause. She did not sit down again beside him, and she did not take the gun he was holding up invitingly to her. She put her hands behind her and stood accusingly before him with the look upon her face which never failed to make sundry small Beckmans and Pilgreens squirm on their benches when she assumed it in school.

"Mr. Davidson"—not Weary Davidson, as she was wont to call him—"you have killed my pet gopher. All summer I have fed him, and he would eat out of my hand."

Weary cast a jealous eye upon the limp, little animal, searched his heart for remorse and found none. Ornery little brute, to get familiar with *his* schoolma'am!

"I did not think you could be so wantonly cruel, and I am astonished and—and deeply pained to discover that fatal flaw in your character."

Weary began to squirm, after the manner of delinquent Beckmans and Pilgreens. One thing he had learned: When the schoolma'am rose to irreproachable English, there was trouble a-brew. It was a sign he had never known to fail.

"I cannot understand the depraved instinct which prompts a man brutally to destroy a life he cannot restore, and which in no way menaces his own—or even interferes with his comfort. You may apologize to me; you may even be sincerely repentant"—the schoolma'am's tone at this point implied considerable doubt—"but you are powerless to return the life you have so heedlessly taken. You have revealed a low, brutal trait which I had hoped your nature could not harbor, and I am—am deeply shocked and—and grieved."

Just here a tiny, dry-weather whirlwind swept around the corner, caught ruffled, white apron and blue skirt in its gyrations and, pushing them wickedly aside, gave Weary a brief, delicious glimpse of two small, slippered feet and two distracting ankles. The schoolma'am blushed and retreated to the doorstep, but she did not sit down. She still stood straight and displeased beside him. Evidently she was still shocked and grieved.

Weary tipped his head to one side so that be might look up at her from under his hat-brim. "I'll get yuh another gopher; six, if yuh say so," he soothed, "The woods is full of 'em."

The angry, brown eyes of Miss Satterly swept the barren hills contemptuously. She would not even look at him. "Pray do not inconvenience yourself, Mr. Davidson. It is not the gopher that I care for so much—it is the principle."

Weary sighed and slid the gun back into his pocket. It seemed to him that Miss Satterly, adorable as she always was, was also rather unreasonable at times. "All right, I'll get yuh another principle, then."

"Mr. Davidson," she said sternly, "you are perfectly odious!"

"Is that something nice, Girlie?" Weary smiled trustfully up at her.

"Odious," explained the schoolma'am haughtily, "is not something nice. I'm sorry your education has been so neglected. Odious, Mr. Davidson, is a synonym for hateful, obnoxious, repulsive, disagreeable, despicable—"

"I never did like cinnamon, anyhow," put in Weary, cheerfully.

"I did not mention cinnamon. I said—"

"Say, yuh look out uh sight with your hair fixed that way. I wish you'd wear it like that all the time," he observed irrelevantly, looking up at her with his sunniest smile.

"I wish to goodness I were really out of sight," snapped the schoolma'am. "You make me exceedingly weary."

"*Mrs.* Weary," corrected he, complacently. "That's what I'm sure aiming at."

"You aim wide of the mark, then," she retorted valiantly, though confusion waved a red flag in either cheek.

"Oh, I don't know. A minute ago you were roasting me because my aim was too good," he contended mildly, glancing involuntarily toward the gopher stretched upon its little, yellow back, its four small feet turned pitifully up to the blue.

"If you had an atom of decency you'd be ashamed to mention that tribute to your diabolical marksmanship."

"Oh, mamma!" ejaculated Weary under his breath, and began to make himself a smoke. His guardian angel was exhorting him to silence, but it preached, as usual, to unsentient ears.

"*I* never mentioned all those things," he denied meekly. "It's you that keeps on mentioning. I wish yuh wouldn't. I like to hear you talk, all right, and flop all those big words easy as roping a calf; but I wish you'd let me choose your subject for yuh. I could easy name one where you could use words just as high and wide and handsome, and a heap more pleasant than the brand you've got corralled. Try admiration and felicitation and exhilarating, ecstatic osculation—" He stopped to run the edge of paper along his tongue, and perhaps it was as well he did; there was no need of making her any angrier. Miss Satterly hated to feel that she was worsted, and it was quite clear that Weary had all along been "guying" her.

"If you came here to make me *hate* you, you have accomplished your errand admirably; it would be advisable now for you to hike."

Weary, struck by that incongruous last word, did an unforgivable thing. He laughed and laughed, while the match he had just lighted flared, sent up a blue thread of brimstone smoke, licked along the white wood and scorched his fingers painfully before he remembered his cigarette.

Miss Satterly turned abruptly and went into the house, put on her hat and took up the little, tin lard-pail in which her aunt Meeker always packed her lunch. She was back, had the key turned in the lock and was slowly pulling on her gloves by the time Weary recovered from his mirth.

"Since you will not leave the place, I shall do so. I want to say first, however, that I not only think you odious, but all the synonyms I mentioned besides. You need not come for me to go to the Labor Day dance, because I will not go with you. I shall go with Joe."

Weary gave her a startled glance and almost dropped his cigarette. This seemed going rather far, he thought—but of course she didn't really mean it; the schoolma'am, he heartened himself with thinking, was an awful, little bluffer.

"Don't go off mad, Girlie. I'm sorry I killed your gopher— on the dead, I am. I just didn't think, That's a habit I've got—not thinking.

"Say! You stay, and we'll have a funeral. It isn't every common, scrub gopher that can have a real funeral with mourners and music when he goes over the Big Divide. He—he'll appreciate the honor; I would, I know, if it was me."

The schoolma'am took a few steps and stopped, evidently in some difficulty with her glove. From the look of her, no human being was within a mile of her; she certainly did not seem to hear anything Weary was saying.

"Say! I'll sing a song over him, if you'll wait a minute. I know two whole verses of 'Bill Bailey,' and the chorus to 'Good Old Summertime.' I can shuffle the two together and make a full deck. I believe they'd go fine together.

"Say, you never heard me sing, did yuh? It's worth waiting for—only yuh want to hang tight to something when I start. Come on—I'll let you be the mourner."

Since Miss Satterly had been taking steps quite regularly while Weary was speaking, she was now several rods away—and she had, more than ever, the appearance of not hearing him and of not wanting to hear.

"Say, Tee-e-cher!"

The schoolma'am refused to stop, or to turn her head a fraction of an inch, and Weary's face sobered a little. It was the first time that inimitable "Tee-e-cher" of his had failed to bring the smile back into the eyes of Miss Satterly. He looked after her dubiously. Her shoulders were thrown well back and her feet pressed their imprint firmly into the yellow dust of the trail. In a minute she would be quite out of hearing.

Weary got up, took a step and grasped Glory's trailing bridle-rein and hurried after her much faster than Glory liked and which he reproved with stiffened knees and a general pulling back on the reins.

"Say! You wouldn't get mad at a little thing like that, would yuh?" expostulated Weary, when he overtook her. "You know I didn't mean anything, Girlie."

"I do not consider it a little thing," said the schoolma'am, icily.

Thus rebuffed, Weary walked silently beside her up the hill—silently, that is, save for the subdued jingling of his spurs. He was beginning to realize that there was an uncomfortable, heavy feeling in his chest, on the side where his heart was. Still, he was of a hopeful nature and presently tried again.

"How many times must I say I'm sorry, Schoolma'am? You don't look so pretty when you're mad; you've got dimples, remember, and yuh ought to give 'em a chance. Let's sit down on this rock while I square myself. Come on." His tone was wheedling in the extreme.

Miss Satterly, not replying a word, kept straight on up the hill; and

Weary, sighing heavily, followed.

"Don't you want to ride Glory a ways? He's real good, to-day. He put in the whole of yesterday working out all the cussedness that's been accumulating in his system for a week, so he's dead gentle. I'll lead him, for yuh."

"Thank you," said Miss Satterly. "I prefer to walk."

Weary sighed again, but clung to his general hopefulness, as was his nature. It took a great deal to rouse Weary; perhaps the schoolma'am was trying to find just how much.

"Say, you'd a died laughing if you'd seen old Glory yesterday; he liked to scared Slim plumb to death. We were working in the big corral and Slim got down on one knee to fix his spur. Glory saw him kneel down, and gave a running jump and went clear over Slim's head. Slim hit for the closest fence, and he never looked back till he was clean over on the other side. Mamma! I was sure amused. I thought Glory had done about everything there was to do—but I tell yuh, that horse has got an imagination that will make him famous some day."

For the first time since the day of his spectacular introduction to her, Miss Satterly displayed absolutely no interest in the eccentricities of Glory. Slowly it began to dawn upon Weary that she did not intend to thaw that evening. He glanced at her sidelong, and his eyes had a certain gleam that was not there five minutes before. He swung along beside her till they reached the top of the hill, fell behind without a word and mounted Glory. When he overtook Miss Satterly, he lifted his hat to her nonchalantly, touched up Glory with his spurs, and clattered away down the coulee, leaving the schoolma'am in a haze of yellow dust and bewilderment far in the rear.

The next morning Miss Satterly went very early to the school-house—for what purpose she did not say. A meadow-lark on the doorstep greeted her with his short, sweet ripple of sound and then flew to a nearby sage bush and watched her curiously. She looked about her half expectant, half disappointed.

A little, fresh mound marked the spot where the dead gopher had been, and a narrow strip of shingle stood upright at the end. Someone had scratched the words with a knife:

GONE BUT NOT FORGOT.

Probably the last word would have been given its full complement of syllables, had the shingle been wider; as it was, the "forgot" was cramped until it was barely intelligible.

Miss Satterly, observing the mark of high-heeled boots in the immediate vicinity of the grave, caught herself wondering if the remains had been laid away to the tune of "Bill Bailey," with the chorus of "Good Old Summertime" shuffled in to make a full deck. She started to laugh and found that laughter was quite impossible.

Suddenly the schoolma'am did a strange thing. She glanced about to make sure no one was in sight, knelt and patted the tiny mound very tenderly; then, stooping quickly, she pressed her lips impulsively upon the rude lettering of the shingle. When she sprang up her cheeks were very red, her eyes dewy and lovely, and the little laugh she gave at herself was all atremble. If lovers could be summoned as opportunely in real life as they are in stories, hearts would not ache so often and life would be quite monotonously serene.

Weary was at that moment twenty miles away, busily engaged in chastising Glory, that had refused point-blank to cross a certain washout. His mind being wholly absorbed in the argument, he was not susceptible to telepathic messages from the Meeker school-house—which was a pity.

Also, it was a pity he could not know that Miss Satterly lingered late at the school-house that night, doing nothing but watch the trail where it lay, brown and distinct and utterly deserted, on the top of the bill a quarter of a mile away. It is true she had artfully scattered a profusion of papers over her desk and would undoubtedly have been discovered hard at work upon them and very much astonished at beholding him—if he had come. It is probable that Weary would have found her quite unapproachable, intrenched behind a bulwark of dignity and correct English.

When the shadow of the schoolhouse stretched somberly away to the very edge of the coulee. Miss Satterly gathered up the studied confusion on her desk, bundled the papers inside, and turned the key with a snap, jabbed three hatpins viciously through her hat and her hair and went home—and perhaps it were well that Weary was not there at that time.

The next night, papers strewed the desk as before, and the schoolma'am stood by the window, her elbows planted on the unpainted sill, and watched the trail listlessly. Her eyes were big and wistful, like a hurt child's, and her cheeks were not red as usual, nor even pink. But the trail lay again brown, and silent, and lonesome, with no quick hoof-beats to send the dust swirling up in a cloud.

The shadows flowed into the coulee until it was full to the brim and threatening the golden hilltop with a brown veil of shade before Miss Satterly locked her door and went home. When she reached her aunt Meeker's she did not want any supper and she said her head ached. But that was not quite true; it was not her head that ached so much; it was her heart.

The third day, the schoolma'am fussed a long time with her hair, which she did in four different styles. The last style was the one which Weary had pronounced "out uh sight"—only she added a white chiffon bow which she had before kept sacred to dances and which Weary always admired. At noon she encouraged the children to gather wild flowers from the coulee, and she filled several tin cans with water from the spring and arranged the bouquets with much care. Weary loved flowers. Nearly every time he came he had a little bunch stuck under his hat-band. A few she put in her hair, along with the chiffon bow. She urged the children through their work and dismissed them at eleven minutes to four and told them to go straight home.

After she had swept the floor and dusted everything that could be dusted so that the school-room had the peculiar, immaculate emptiness and forlornness, like a church on a week day, and had taken a few of the brightest flowers and pinned them upon her white shirt-waist. Miss Satterly tuned her guitar in minor and went out and sat upon the shady doorstep and waited frankly, strumming plaintive little airs while she watched the trail. To-morrow was Labor Day, and so he would certainly ride over to-night to see if she had really meant it (Miss Satterly did not explain to herself what "it" was; surely, there was no need).

At half-past five—Miss Satterly had looked at her watch seventeen times during the interval—a tiny cloud of dust rose over the brow of the hill, and her heart danced in her chest until she could scarce breathe.

The cloud grew and grew and began drifting down the trail, and behind it a black something rose over the hilltop and followed it, so proclaiming itself a horseman galloping swiftly towards her. The color spread from the schoolma'am's cheeks to her brow and throat. Her fingers forgot their cunning and plucked harrowing discords from the strings, but her lips were parted and smiling tremulously. It was late—she had almost given up looking—but he was coming! She knew be would come. Coming at a breakneck pace—he must be pretty anxious, too. The schoolma'am recovered a bit of control and revolved in her mind several pert forms of greeting. She would not be too ready to forgive him—it would do him good to keep him anxious and uncertain for a while before she gave in.

Now he was near the place where he would turn off the main road and gallop straight to her. Glory always made that turn of his own accord, lately. Weary had told her, last Sunday, how he could never get Glory past that turn, any more, without a fight, no matter what might be the day or the hour.

Now he would swing into the school-house trail. Miss Satterly raised both hands with a very feminine gesture and patted her hair tentatively, tucking in a stray lock here and there.

Her hands dropped heavily to her lap, just as the blood dropped away from her cheeks and the happy glow dulled in her eyes. It was not Weary. It was the Swede who worked for Jim Adams and who rode a sorrel horse which, at a distance, resembled Glory.

Mechanically she watched him go on down the trail and out of sight; picked up her guitar which had grown suddenly heavy, crept inside and closed the door and locked it She looked around the clean, eerily silent schoolroom, walked with echoing steps to the desk and laid her head down among the cans of sweet-smelling, prairie flowers and cried softly, in a tired, heartbreaking fashion that made her throat ache, and her head.

The shadows had flowed over the coulee-rim and the hilltops were smothered in gloom when Miss Satterly went home that night, and her aunt Meeker sent her straight to bed and dosed her with horrible home remedies.

By morning she had recovered her spirit—her revengeful spirit, which she kept as the hours wore on and Weary did not come. She would teach him a lesson, she told herself often. By evening, however, her mood softened. There were many things that could have kept him away against his will; he was not his own master, and it was shipping time. Probably he had been out with the roundup, or something. She decided that petty revenge is unwomanly besides giving evidence of a narrow mind and shallow, and if Weary could show a good and sufficient reason for staying away like that when there were matters to be settled between them, she would not be petty and mean about it; she would be divine—and forgive.

PART THREE

Weary was standing pensively by the door, debating with himself the advisability of going boldly over and claiming the first waltz with the schoolma'am—and taking a chance on being refused—when Cal Emmett gave him a vicious poke in the ribs by way of securing his attention.

"Do yuh see that bunch uh red loco over there by the organ?" he wanted to know. "That's Bert Rogers' cousin from Iowa."

Weary looked and wilted against the wall. "Oh, Mamma!" he gasped.

"Ain't she a peach? There'll be more than one pair uh hands go into the air to-night. It's a good thing Len got the drop on me first or I'd be making seven kinds of a fool uh myself, chances is. Bert says she's bad medicine—a man-killer from away back.

"Say, she's giving us the bad-eye. Don't rubber like that, Weary; it ain't good manners, and besides; the schoolma'am's getting fighty, if I'm any judge."

Weary pulled himself together and tried to look away, but a pair of long blue eyes with heavy white lids drew him hypnotically across the room. He did not want to go; he did not mean to go, but the first he knew he was standing before her and she was smiling up at him just as she used to do. And an evil spell seemed to fall upon Weary, so that he thought one set of thoughts while his lips uttered sentences quite apart from his wishes. He was telling her, for instance, that he was glad to see her; and he was not glad. He was wishing the train which brought her to

Montana had jumped the track and gone over a high cut-bank, somewhere.

She continued to smile up at him, and she called him Will and held out her hand. When, squirming inward protest, he took it, she laid her left hand upon his and somehow made him feel as if he were in a trap. Her left hand was soft and plump and cool, and it was covered with rings that gave flashes and sparkles of light when she moved, and her nails were manicured to a degree not often seen in Dry Lake. She drew her fingers caressingly over his hand and spoke to him in *italics*, in the way that had made many a man lose his head and say things extremely foolish. Her name was Myrtle Forsyth, as Weary had cause to remember.

"How strange to see you away out here," she murmured, and glanced to where the musicians were beginning to play little preparatory strains. "Have you forgotten how to *waltz*, Will? You used to dance so *well*!"

What could a man do after a hint as broad as that one? Weary held out his arm meekly, while mentally he was gnashing his teeth, and muttered something about her giving him a trial. And she slipped her hand under his elbow with a proprietary air that was not lost upon a certain brown-eyed young woman across the hall.

Weary had said some hard things to Myrtle Forsyth when he talked with her last, away back in Iowa; he had hoped to heaven he never would see her again. Now, she observed that he had not lost his good looks in grieving over her. She decided that he was even better looking;

there was an air of strength and a self poise that was very becoming to his broad shoulders and the six feet two inches of his height. She thought, before the waltz was over, that she had made a mistake when she threw him over—a mistake which she ought to rectify at once.

Weary never knew how she managed it—in truth, he was not aware that she did it at all—but he seemed to dance a great many times with her of the long eyes and the bright auburn hair. The schoolma'am seemed always to be at the farther end of the room, and she appeared to be enjoying herself very much and to dance incessantly.

Once he broke away from Miss Forsyth and went and asked Miss Satterly for the next waltz; but she opened her big eyes at him and assured him politely that she was engaged. He tried for a quadrille, a two-step, a schottische—even for a polka, which she knew he hated; but the schoolma'am was, apparently, the most engaged young woman in Dry Lake that night.

So Weary owned himself beaten and went back to Miss Forsyth, who had been watching and learning many things and making certain plans. Weary danced with her once and took a fit of sulking, when he stood over by the door and smoked cigarettes and watched moodily the whirling couples. Miss Forsyth drifted to other acquaintances, which was natural; what was not so natural, to Weary's mind, was to see her sitting out a quadrille with the schoolma'am.

That did not look good to Weary, and he came near going over and demanding to know what they were talking about. He was ready to bet that Myrt Forsyte, with that smile, was up to some deviltry—and he wished he knew what. She reminded him somewhat of Glory when Glory was cloyed with peaceful living. He even told himself viciously that Myrt Forsyth had hair the exact shade of Glory's, and it came near giving him a dislike of the horse. The conversation in the corner, after certain conventional subjects had been exhausted, came to Miss Forsyth's desire something like this: She said how she loved to waltz,—with the right partner, that is. Apropos the right partner, she glanced slyly from the end of her long eyes and remarked:

"Will—Mr. Davidson—is an *ideal* partner, don't you think? Are you—but of *course* you must be *acquainted* with him, living in the same *neighborhood?*" Her inflection made a question of the declaration.

"Certainly I am acquainted with Mr. Davidson," said Miss Satterly with just the right shade of indifference. "He does dance very well, though there are others I like better." That, of course, was a prevarication. "You knew him before tonight?"

Miss Forsyth laughed that sort of laugh which may mean anything you like. "*Knew* him? Why, we were en—that is, we grew *up* in the same *town*. I was so perfectly *amazed* to find him *here*, poor fellow."

"Why poor fellow?" asked Miss Satterly, the direct. "Because you found him? or because he is here?"

The long eyes regarded her curiously. "Why, don't you *know*?

Hasn't—hasn't it *followed* him?"

"I don't know, I'm sure," said the schoolma'am, calmly facing the stare. "If you mean a dog, he doesn't own one, I believe. Cowboys don't seem to take to dogs; they're afraid they might be mistaken for sheep-herders, perhaps—and that would be a disgrace."

Miss Forsyth leaned back and her eyes, half closed as they were, saw Weary away down by the door. "No, I didn't mean a *dog*. I'm *glad* if he has gotten *quite away* from— he's such a *dear* fellow! Even if he *did*—but I never believed it, you know. If only he had *trusted* me, and *stayed* to face— But he went without telling me *goodbye*, even, and we— But he was *afraid*, you see—"

Miss Satterly also glanced across to where Weary stood gloomily alone, his hands thrust into his pockets. "I really can't imagine Mr. Davidson as being afraid," she remarked defensively.

"Oh, but you don't understand! Will is *physically* brave— and he was afraid I— but I *believed* in him, *always*—even when—" She broke off suddenly and became prettily diffident. "I wonder *why* I am talking to *you* like this. But there is something so *sympathetic* in your very *atmosphere*—and seeing *him* so *unexpectedly* brought it all *back*—and it seemed as if I *must* talk to *someone*, or I should *shriek*." (Myrtle Forsyth was often just upon the point of "shrieking") "And he was *so* glad to see me—and when I *told* him I never *believed* a *word*— But you see, *leaving* the way he *did*—"

"Well," said Miss Satterly rather unsympathetically, "and how did he leave, then?"

Miss Forsyth twisted her watch chain and hesitated. "I really ought *not* to say a *word*—if you really don't *know*—what he *did*—"

"If it's to his discredit," said the schoolma'am, looking straight at her, "I certainly don't know. It must have been something awful, judging from your tone. Did he"—she spoke solemnly—"did he _mur-r_der ten people, old men and children, and throw their bodies into—a *well*?"

It is saying much for Miss Forsyth that she did not look as disconcerted as she felt. She did, however, show a rather catty look in her eyes, and her voice was tinged faintly with malice. "There are *other* crimes—beside—*murder*," she reminded. "I won't tell *what* it was—but—but *Will* found it necessary to *leave in the night*! He did not even come to tell *me* goodbye, and I have—but now we have met by *chance*, and I could *explain*—and so," she smiled tremulously at the schoolma'am, "I *know* you can *understand*—and you will not *mention* to *anyone* what I have told you. I'm too *impulsive*—and I felt *drawn* to you, somehow. I—I would *die* if I thought any *harm* could come to Will because of my *confiding* in you. A woman," she added pensively, "has so *much* to bear—and this has been very *hard*—because it was not a thing I could *talk over*—not even with my own *mother*!" Miss Forsyth had the knack of saying very little that was definite, and implying a great deal. This method saved her the unpleasantness of retraction, and had quite as deep an effect is if she came out plainly. She smiled confidingly down at the schoolma'am and went off to waltz with Bert Rogers, apparently quite satisfied with what she had accomplished.

Miss Satterly sat very still, scarce thinking consciously. She stared at Weary and tried to imagine him a fugitive from his native town, and in spite of herself wondered what it was he had done. It must be something very bad, and she shrank from the thought. Then Cal Emmett came up to ask her for a dance, and she went with him thankfully and tried to forget the things she had heard.

Weary, after dancing with every woman but the one he wanted, and finding himself beside Myrtle Forsyth with a frequency that puzzled him, felt an unutterable disgust for the whole thing. After a waltz quadrille, during which he seemed to get her out of his arms only to find her swinging into them again, and smiling up at him in a way he knew of old, he made desperately for the door; snatched up the first gray hat he came to—which happened to belong to Chip—and went out into the dewy darkness.

It was half an hour before he could draw the hostler of the Dry Lake stable away from a crap game, and it was another half hour before he succeeded in overcoming Glory's disinclination for a gallop over the prairie alone. But it was two hours before Miss Forsythe gave over watching furtively the door, and it was daylight before

Chip Emmett found a gray hat under the water bench—a hat which he finally recognized as Weary's and so appropriated to his own use.

PART FOUR

Weary clattered up to the school-house door to find it erupting divers specimens of young America—by adoption, some of them. He greeted each one cheerfully by name and waited upon his horse in the shade.

Close behind the last sun-bonnet came Miss Satterly, key in hand. Evidently she had no intention of lingering, that night; Weary smiled down upon her tentatively and made a hasty guess as to her state of mind—a very important factor in view of what he had come to say.

"It's awful hot, Schoolma'am; if I were you I'd wait a while—till the sun lets up a little."

To his unbounded surprise, Miss Satterly calmly sat down upon the doorstep. Weary promptly slid out of the saddle and sat down beside her, thankful that the step was not a wide one. "You've been unmercifully hard to locate since the dance," he complained. "I like to lost my job, chasing over this way, when I was supposed to be headed another direction. I came by here last night at five minutes after four, and you weren't in sight anywhere; was yesterday a holiday?"

"You probably didn't look in the window," said the schoolma'am. "I was writing letters here till after five."

"With the door shut and locked?"

"The wind blew so," explained Miss Satterly, lamely. "And that lock—"

"First I knew of the wind blowing yesterday. It was as hot as the hubs uh he—as blue blazes when I came by. There weren't any windows up, even—I hope you was real comfortable."

"Perfectly," she assured him.

"I'll gamble yuh were! Well, and where were yuh cached last Sunday?"

"Nowhere. I went with Bert and Miss Forsyth up in the mountains. We took our lunch and had a perfectly lovely time."

"I'm glad somebody had a good time. I got away at nine o'clock and came over to Meeker's—and you weren't there; so I rode the rim-rocks till sundown, trying to locate yuh. It's easier hunting strays in the Bad Lands."

Miss Satterly seemed about to speak, but she changed her mind and gazed at the coulee-rim.

"It's hard to get away, these days," Weary went on explaining. "I wanted to come before the dance, but we were gathering some stuff out the other way, and I couldn't. The Old Man is shipping, yuh see; we're holding a bunch right now, waiting for cars. I got Happy Jack to stand herd in my place, is how I got here."

The schoolma'am yawned apologetically into her palm. Evidently she was not greatly interested in the comings and goings of Weary Davidson.

"How did yuh like the dance?" he asked, coming to the subject that he knew was the vital point.

"Lovely," said the schoolma'am briefly, but with fervor.

"Different here," asserted Weary. "I drifted, right before supper."

"*Did* you?" Miss Satterly accented the first word in a way she taught her pupils indicated surprise. "I don't reckon you noticed it. You were pretty busy, about then." Miss Satterly laughed languid assent.

"I never knew before that Bert Rogers was any relation of Myrt Forsyth," observed Weary, edging still nearer the vital point. "They sure aren't much alike."

"You used to know her?" asked Miss Satterly, politely.

"Well, I should say yes. I used to go to school with Myrt. How do you like her?"

"Lovely," said Miss Satterly, this time without fervor.

Weary began digging a trench with his spurs. He wished the schoolma'am would not limit herself so rigidly to that one adjective. It became unmeaning with much use, so that it left a fellow completely in the dark.

"Just about everybody says that about her—at first," he remarked.

"Did you?" she asked him, still politely.

"I did a heap worse than that," said Weary, grimly determined. "I had a bad case of calf-love and made a fool uh myself generally."

"What fun!" chirped the schoolma'am with an unconvincing little laugh.

"Not for me, it wasn't. Whilst I had it I used to pack a lock uh that red hair in my breast pocket and heave sighs over it that near lifted me out uh my boots. Oh, I was sure earnest! But she did me the biggest favor she could; a slick-haired piano-tuner come to town and she turned me down for him. I was plumb certain my heart was busted wide open, at the time, though." Weary laughed reminiscently.

"She said—I think you misunderstood her. She appears to—" Miss Satterly, though she felt that she was being very generous, did not quite know how to finish.

"Not on your life! It was the first time I ever did understand Myrt.

When I left there I wasn't doing any guessing."

"You shouldn't have left," she told him suddenly; gripping her courage at this bold mention of his flight. How she wished she knew why he left.

"Oh, I don't know. It was about the only thing I could do, at the time—the only thing, that is, that I wanted to do. It seemed like I couldn't get away fast enough." It was brazen of him, she thought, to treat it all so coolly. "And out here," he added thoughtfully, "I could get the proper focus on Myrt—which I couldn't do back there."

"Distance lends—"

"Not in this case," he interrupted. "It's when you're right with Myrt that she kinda hypnotizes yuh into thinking what she wants yuh to think." He was remembering resentfully the dance.

"But to sneak away—"

"That's a word I don't remember was ever shot at me before," said Weary, the blood showing through the skin on his cheeks. "If that damned Myrt has been telling yuh—"

"I didn't think you would speak like that about a woman, Mr. Davidson," said the schoolma'am with disapproval in her tone; and the disapproval not going very deep, there was the more of it upon the surface.

"I suppose it gives evidence of a low, brutal trait in my nature, that you hoped I couldn't harbor," acceded Weary meekly.

"It does," snapped the schoolma'am, her cheeks hot. If she had repented her flare of temper over the gopher, she certainly did not intend letting him know it too soon. She seemed inclined to discipline him a bit.

Weary smoked silently and raked up the sun-baked soil with his spurs.

"How long is Myrt going to stay?" he ventured at last.

"I never asked her," she retorted. "You ought to know— you probably have seen her last." The schoolma'am blundered, there.

Weary drew a sigh of relief; if she were jealous, it must mean that she cared. "That's right. I saw her last night," he stated calmly.

Miss Satterly sat more erect, if that were possible. She had not known of this last meeting, and she had merely shot at random, anyway.

"At least," he amended, watching her from the corner of his eye, "I saw a woman and a man ride over the hill back of Denson's, last night. The man was Bert, and the woman had red hair; I took it to be Myrt."

"You surely should be a good judge," remarked Miss Satterly, irritated because she knew he was teasing.

Weary was quick to read the signs. "What did you mean, a while back, about me sneaking away from Chadville? And how did yuh happen to have your dances booked forty-in-advance, the other night? And what makes yuh so mean to me, lately? And will yuh take a jaunt over Eagle Butte way with me next Sunday—if I can get off?"

The schoolma'am, again feeling herself mistress of the situation, proceeded with her disciplining. She smiled, raised one hand and checked off the questions upon her fingers. You never would guess how oddly her heart was behaving—she looked such a self-possessed young woman.

"I'll begin at the last one and work backward," she said, calmly. "And I must hurry, for aunt Meeker hates to keep supper waiting. No, I will *not* go for a jaunt over Eagle Butte way next Sunday. I have other plans; if I *hadn't* other plans I still would not go. I hope this is quite plain to you?"

"Oh, it's good and plain," responded Weary. "But for the Lord's sake don't take up that talking in italics like Myrt does. I can't stand this bearing down hard on every other word. It sets my teeth all on edge."

The schoolma'am opened her eyes wider. Was it possible Weary was acquiring an irritable temper? "*Second*," she went on deliberately, "I do not *consider* that I have been *mean* to you; and if I *have* it is because I *choose* to be so."

Weary, observing a most flagrant accent, shut his lips rather tightly together.

"Third—let me see. Oh, that about the *dances*; I can only say that we *women*, as a means of *self-defence*, claim the privilege of *effacing* undesirable, would-be partners by a certain *form* of rejection, which *eliminates* the necessity of going into unpleasant *details*, and—er—lets the fellow down easy." The schoolma'am's emphasis and English seemed to collapse together, but Weary did not notice that.

"I'm sure grateful to be let down easy," he said softly, without looking up; his head was bent so that his hat quite concealed from the schoolma'am his face, but if she had known him longer, perhaps she would have gone carefully after that.

"As to your sneaking away from—wherever it was—surely, you ought to know about that better than I do. One must go far to outdistance dishonor, for a man's misdeeds are sure to follow him, soon or late. I will not go into details—but you understand what I mean."

"No," said Weary, still with bent head, "I'll be darned if I do. And if I did, I know about where to locate the source of all the information you've loaded up on. Things were going smooth as silk till Myrt Forsyth drifted out here—the red-headed little devil!"

"Mr. Davidson!" cried the schoolma'am, truly shocked.

"Oh, I'm revealing some more low, brutal instincts, I expect I'm liable to reveal a lot more if I hang around much longer." He stopped, as if there was more he wanted to say, and was doubtful of the wisdom of saying it.

"I came over to say something—something particular—but I've changed my mind. I guess yuh haven't much time to listen, and I don't believe it would interest yuh as much as I thought it would—a while back. You just go ahead and make a bosom friend uh Myrt Forsyth, Schoolma'am, and believe every blamed lie she tells yuh. I won't be here to argue the point. Looks to me like I'm about due to drift."

Miss Satterly, dumb with fear of what his words might mean, sat stiffly while Weary got up and mounted Glory in a business like manner that was extremely disquieting.

"I wish you could a cared, Girlie," he said with a droop of his unsmiling mouth and a gloom in his eyes when he looked at her. "I was a chump, I reckon, to ever imagine yuh could. Good-bye—and be good to—yourself." He leaned to one side, swung backward his feet and Glory, obeying the signal, wheeled and bounded away.

Miss Satterly watched him gallop up the long slope and the pluckety pluckety of Glory's fleeing feet struck heavy, numbing blows upon her heart. She wondered why she had refused to ride with him, when she did want to go— she did. And why had she been so utterly hateful, after waiting and watching, night after night, for him to come? And just how much did he mean by being due to drift? He couldn't be really angry—and what was he going to say— the thing he changed his mind about. Was it—Well, he would come again in a few days, and then—

PART FIVE

Weary did not go back. When the hurry of shipping was over he went to Shorty and asked for his time, much to the foreman's astonishment and disgust. The Happy Family was incensed and wasted profanity and argument trying to make him give up the crazy notion of quitting. It seemed to Weary that he warded off their curiosity and answered their arguments very adroitly. He was sick of punching cows, he said, and he wasn't hankering for a chance to shovel hay another winter to an ungrateful bunch of bawling calves. He was going to drift, for a change—but he didn't know where. It didn't much matter, so long as he got a change uh scenery. He just merely wanted to knock around and get the alkali dust out of his lungs and see something grow besides calves and cactus. His eyes plumb ached for sight of an apple tree with real, live apples on it—that weren't wrapped up in a paper napkin.

When was he coming back? Well, now, that was a question; he hadn't got started yet, man. What he was figuring on wasn't the coming back part, but the getting started.

The schoolma'am? Oh, he guessed she could get along without him, all right. Seeing they mentioned her, would some of them tell her hello for him—and so long?

This last was at the station, where they had ridden in a body to see him off. Weary waved his hat as long as the town was in sight, and the Happy Family ran their horses to keep pace with the train when it pulled out, emptied their six-shooters into the air and yelled parting words till the Pullman windows were filled with shocked, Eastern faces, eager to see a real, wild cowboy on his native soil. Then Weary went into the smoker, sought a place where he could stretch the long legs of him over two seats, made him a cigarette and forgot to smoke it while he watched the gray plains slide away behind him; till something went wrong with his eyes. It was just four o'clock, and school was out. The schoolma'am was looking down the trail, maybe— At any rate she was a good many miles away from him now—so many that even if he got off and had Glory right there and ran him every foot of the way, he could not possibly get to her—and the way the train was galloping over the rails, she was every minute getting farther off, and— What a damn fool a man can make of himself, rushing off like that when, maybe—

After that, a fellow who traveled for a San Francisco wine house spoke to him pleasantly and Weary thrust vain longings from him and was himself again.

For two months he wandered aimlessly and, then, not quite at the point of going back and not being rich or an idler by nature, he started out, one gloomy morning in late November, looking for work. He was in Portland and the city was strange to him, for he had dropped off a north-bound train the night before.

People hurried past without a glance in his direction, and even after two months this made him lonesome, coming as he did from a place where every man hailed him jovially by his adopted name.

There was little that he could do—or would do. He tried digging ditches for the city, along with a motley collection of the sons of all nations but his, seemingly.

The first day be blistered both hands and got a "crick" in his back.

The second day, he quit.

On the third day, he brought up at the door of a livery stable. A man with a slate-colored, silk waistcoat was standing aggressively in the doorway, one hand deep in his pocket and the other energetically punctuating the remarks he was making to a droop-shouldered hostler. Some of the remarks were interesting in the extreme and Weary, listening, drew a deep sigh of thankfulness that they were not directed at himself, because his back was still lame and his hands sore, and in Portland law-abiding citizens are not supposed to "pack" a gun.

The droop-shouldered man waited humbly for the climax—which reached so high a tension that the speaker rose upon his toes to deliver it, and drew his right hand from his pocket to aid in the punctuation—when he pulled his hat down on his head and slunk away.

It was while the orator was gazing contemptuously after him that he heard Weary cheerfully asking for work. For Weary was a straight guesser; he knew when he stood in the presence of the Great and Only. The man wheeled and measured Weary slowly with his eyes—and there being a good deal of Weary if you measured lengthwise, he consumed several seconds doing it.

"Humph!" when the survey was over. "What do *you* know about horses?" His tone was colored still by the oration he had just delivered, and it was not encouraging.

Weary looked down upon him and smiled indulgence of the tone. "If you aren't busy right now, I'll start in and tell yuh. Yuh better sit down on that bucket whilst I'm doing it—if I'm thorough it'll take time."

"Humph!" said the man again and carefully pared the end of a fat, black cigar. "You seem to think you know it all. What's your trade?"

"Punching cows—in Northern Montana," answered Weary, mildly.

The man took the trouble to look at him again, this time more critically—and more favorably, perhaps. "Bronco-buster?" he demanded, briefly.

"Some," grinned Weary, his thoughts whirling back to the dust and uproar in the Flying U corrals—and to Glory.

The man seemed to read what was in his eyes. "You ought to know better than to founder a three-hundred-dollar trotter, then," he remarked, with some of the growl smoothed out of his voice.

"I sure had," agreed Weary, sympathetically.

"That's why I fired that four-or-five-kinds-of idiot just now," confided the other, rising to the sympathy in Weary's tone. "I need men that know a little something about horses—the foreman can't always be at a man's elbow. You can start right in—pay's good. Go tell the foreman I've hired you; that's him back there in the office."

Then came the rain. Week after week of drab clouds and drizzle, and no sun to hearten a man for his work. Week after week of bobbing umbrellas, muddy crossings, sloppy pavements and dripping eaves—and a cold that chilled the marrow in his bones.

Weary, after a week of poking along in the rain of an evening when his work was done, threw up his hands, figuratively, and bought him an umbrella, hoping devoutly they would never get to hear of it in Dry Lake. He stood for two minutes in the deep doorway of the store before he found nerve to open the awkward thing, and when he did so he glanced sheepishly around him as if it were a weak thing to do and a disgraceful.

Fog and rain and mud and mist, day after day through long months. Feeding hungry horses their breakfast at five o'clock in the morning; brushing, currying, combing till they shone satin-smooth. Harnessing, unharnessing; washing mud from rigs that would be splashed and plastered again before night. Driving to houses that were known by the number over the door, giving the reins over to somebody and walking back in the rain. Piling mangers with hay, strewing the stalls deep with straw. Patting this horse as he passed, commanding the next to move over, stopping to whisper caressing words into the ear of a favorite. Sitting listlessly in the balcony of some theatre in the evening while a mimic world lived its joys and sorrows below and an orchestra played soft accompaniment to his vagrant thoughts. All this was Weary's life in Portland.

Not exactly hilarious, that life. Not a homelike one to a man fresh from eating, sleeping, working, reveling with fellows who would cheerfully give him the coat upon their straight backs if he needed it; fight for him, laugh at him, or laugh with him, tease him, bully him, love him like a brother—in short, fresh from Jim Whitmore's Happy Family.

No one hailed him as Weary; his fellow hostlers called him simply Bill. No one knew the life he knew or loved the things he loved. His stories of wild rides and hard drives must be explained as he went along and fell even then upon barren soil; so he gave up telling them. Even his speech, colored as it was with the West which lies East of the Cascades, sounded strange in their ears and set him apart. They referred to him as "the cowboy".

Sometimes, when the skies were leaden and the dead atmosphere pressed his very soul to the dank earth, Weary would hoist his umbrella and walk and walk and walk, till the streets grew empty around him and his footsteps sounded hollow on the pavements. One Sunday when it was not actually raining he hired a horse and rode into the country—and he came back draggled and unhappy from plodding through the mud, and he never repeated the experiment.

Sometimes he would sit all the evening in his damp-walled room and smoke cigarettes and wonder what the boys were doing, down in the bunk-house at home. He wondered if they kept Glory up—or if he was rustling on the range, his sorrel back humped to the storms and the deviltry gone out of him with the grim battle for mere life. Perhaps there was a dance somewhere; it was a cinch they would all be there—and Happy Jack would wear the same red necktie and the same painful smile of embarrassment, and there would be a squabble over the piece of bar mirror to shave by. And the schoolma'am— But here Weary's thoughts would shy and stop abruptly, and if it were not too late he would put on his hat and go to a show; one of those ten-cent continuous-performance places, where the Swede and the Dutchman flourish and the Boneless Man ties himself in knots.

A man will grow accustomed to anything, give him time enough. When four months had passed in this fashion, Weary began insensibly to turn more to the present and less often, to the past. His work was not hard, the pay was good and he learned the ways of the town and got more in touch with his acquaintances. They came to fill his life, so that he thought less often of Chip and Cal and Happy Jack and Slim. Others were gradually taking their places.

No one had as yet come to lift Miss Satterly's brown eyes from the deep places of his heart, because he again shied at women; but he was able to draw a veil before them so that they did not haunt him so much. He began to whistle once more, as he went about his work; but he never whistled "Good Old Summertime." There were other foolish songs become popular; he rather fancied "Navajo" these days.

It was past April Fool's day, and Weary was singing "Nava, Nava, my Navajo," melodiously while he spread the straw bedding with his fork. It was a beastly day, even for that climate, but he was glad of it. He had only to fill a dozen mangers and his morning's work was done, with the prospect of an idle forenoon; for no one would want to drive, today, unless it was absolutely necessary.

  "I have a love for-r you that will grow-ow;
  If you'll have a coon for a beau—"
trilled Weary, and snapped the wires off a bale of hay and tore it open, in a hurry to finish.

A familiar, pungent odor smote his nostrils and he straightened. For a minute he stood perfectly still; then his fingers groped tremblingly in the hay, closed upon something, and every nerve in him quivered. He held it fast in his shaking hands and sat down weakly upon the torn bale.

It was a branch off a sage bush—dry, shapeless, bruised in the press, but it carried its message bravely. Holding it close to his face, drinking in the smell of it greedily, he closed his eyes involuntarily.

Great, gray plains closed in upon him—dear, familial plains, scarred and broken with sharp-nosed hills and deep, water-worn coulees gleaming barren and yellow in the sun. The blue, blue sky was bending down to meet the hills, with feathery, white clouds trailing lazily across. His cheeks felt the cool winds which flapped his hat-brim and tingled his blood. His knees pressed the throb and life, the splendid, working muscles of a galloping horse.

Weary's head went down upon his hands, with the bit of sage pressed hard against his cheek.

Now he was racing over the springy sod which sent a sweet, grassy smell up to meet him. Wild range cattle lumbered out of his way, ran a few paces and stopped to gaze after him with big, curious eyes. Before him stood the white-tented camp of the round-up, and the rope corral was filled with circling horses half hidden by the veil of dust thrown upward by their restless, trampling hoofs. Now he was in the midst of them, a coil of rope in his left hand; his right swung the loop circling over his head. And the choking dust was in his eyes and throat, and in his nostrils the rank odor of many horses. Men were shouting to one another above the confusion. Oaths were hurled after a horse which warily dodged the rope. Saddles strewed the ground, bits clanked, spurs jingled, care-free laughs brightened the clamor.

The scene shifted. He was sitting, helpless, in the saddle while Glory carried him wantonly over the hills, shaking his head to make the broken bridle rattle. Now he was stopping in front of a vine-covered porch, where a girl lay sleeping in a hammock—a girl with soft, dark hair falling down to the floor in a heavy braid. Again, he was sitting on the school-house steps, holding a smoking gun in his hand, and the schoolma'am was standing, flushed and reproving, before him. The wind came and fluttered her skirts—

"What's the matter, Bill? Yuh sick?"

Weary raised a white, haggard face. The plains, the blue sky, the sunshine, the wind, the girl—were gone. He was sitting upon a torn bale of hay in a livery stable in Portland. Through the wide, open door he could see the muddy street. Gray water-needles darted incessantly up from the pavement where the straight lines of rain struck. On the roof the rain was drumming a monotone. In his fingers was a crumpled bit of gray sage-brush.

"Sick, Bill?" repeated the foreman, sympathetically.

"Oh, go to hell!" said Weary, ungratefully. He felt tired, and weak and old. He wanted to be left alone. He wanted—God, how he wanted the dream to come back to him, and to come back to him true! To close about him and wrap him in its sunny folds; to steep his senses in the light and the life, the sound and the smell of the plains; to hear the wind rushing over the treeless hills; to see the wild range cattle nosing the crisp, prairie grass.

He got unsteadily upon his legs and went slowly to his room; dropped wearily upon the bed, and buried his face in the pillow like a hurt child. In his fingers he clutched a pungent, gray weed.

PART SIX

Late that night Weary, his belongings stuffed hurriedly into the suit-case he called his "war-bag," started home; so impatient he had a childish desire to ride upon the engine so that he might arrive the sooner, and failing that he spent much of his time lurching between smoking car and tourist sleeper, unable to sit quietly in any place for longer than ten minutes or so. In his coat pocket, where his fingers touched it often, was a crumpled bit of sage-brush. Dry it was, and the gray leaves were crumbling under the touch of his homesick fingers, but the smell of it, aromatic and fresh and strong, breathed of the plains he loved.

At Kalispell he went out on the platform and filled his lungs again and again with Montana air, that was clean of fog and had a nip to it. The sun shone, the sky was blue and the clouds reminded him of a band of new-washed sheep scattered and feeding quietly. The wind blew keen in his face and set his blood a-dance, his blood, which for long months had moved sluggishly in his veins.

At Shelby, a half-dozen cowboys galloped briefly into view as the train whizzed by down the valley, and Weary raised the car window and leaned far out to gaze after them with hungry eyes. He wanted to swing his hat and give a whoop that would get the last wisps of fog and gray murk out of his system—but there were other passengers already shivering and eyeing him in unfriendly fashion because of the open window. He wanted to get out and run and run bareheaded, over the bleak, brown hills; but he closed the window and behaved as well as he could. The stars came out and winked at him just as they used to do when he sat on Meeker's front porch and listened to the schoolma'am singing softly in the hammock, her guitar tinkling a mellow undertone. It was too early now for the hammock to be swinging in the porch. School must be started again, though, and seeing the schoolma'am lived right there with her aunt Meeker, they weren't likely to hire another teacher.

He hoped Myrt Forsyth had gone back to Chadville where she belonged. He wished now that he had written to some of the boys and kept posted on what was happening. He had never sent back so much as a picture postal, and he had consequently not heard a word. But Weary's nature was ever hopeful except when he was extremely angry, and then he did not care much about anything. So now, he took it for granted things had gone along smoothly and that nothing would be changed.

* * * * *

Miss Satterly had just finished listlessly hearing the last spelling class recite, when she glanced through the window and saw Glory, bearing a familiar figure, race down the hill and whip into the school-house path. Her heart gave a flop, so that she caught at the desk to steady her and she felt the color go out of her face. Then her presence of mind returned so that she said "School's dismissed"—without going through the form of "Attention, turn, stand, pass."

The children eyed her curiously, hesitated and then rushed noisily out, and she sank down upon a bench and covered her face with her hands. It was queer that she could not seem to get hold of herself and be calm; it was disgraceful that she should tremble so. Outside she could hear them shouting, "Hello, Weary!" in a dozen different keys, and each time her blood jumped. Her eyes had not tricked her, then—though it was not the first time she had trembled to see a sorrel horse gallop down that hill, and then turned numb when came disillusionment. Would those children never start home? By degrees their shrill voices sounded further away, and the place grew still. But the schoolma'am kept her face covered.

Spurred heels clanked on the threshold, stopped there, and the door shut with a slam. But she did not look up; she did not dare.

Steps came down the room toward her—long, hurrying steps, determined steps. Close beside her they stopped, and for a space that seemed to her long minutes there was no sound.

"Say hello to me—won't you, Girlie?" said a wistful voice that thrilled to the tips of the schoolma'am's shaking fingers. She dropped her hands then, reluctantly. Her lips quivered as Weary had never before seen them do.

"Hello," she obeyed, faintly.

He stood for a moment, studying her face.

"Look up here, Schoolma'am," he commanded at last. "I hate to have my feet get so much attention. I've come back to fight it out—to a finish, this time. Yuh can't stampede me again—look up here. I've been plumb sick for a sight of those big eyes of yours."

Miss Satterly persisted in gazing at the boots of Weary. "Well, are yuh going to?" There was a new, masterful note in Weary's voice, that the schoolma'am felt but did not quite understand—then. She did not, perhaps, realize how plainly her whole attitude spoke surrender.

Weary waited what seemed to him a reasonable time, but her lashes drooped lower, if anything. Then he made one of the quick, unlooked-for moves which made him a master of horses. Before she quite knew what was occurring, the schoolma'am was upon her feet and snuggled close in Weary's eager arms. More, he had a hand under her chin, her face was tilted back and he was smiling down into her wide, startled eyes.

"I didn't burn a streak a thousand miles long in the atmosphere, getting back here, to be scared out now by a little woman like you," he remarked, and tucked a stray, brown lock solicitously behind her ear. Then he bent and kissed her deliberately upon the mouth.

"Now, say you're my little schoolma'am. Quick, before I do it again." He threatened with his lips, and he looked as if he were quite anxious to carry out his threat.

"I'm your—" the schoolma'am hid her face from him. "Oh, Will! Whatever made you go off like that, and I—I nearly died wanting to see you—"

Weary laid his cheek very tenderly against hers, and held her close. No words came to either, just then.

"What if I'd kept on being a fool—and hadn't come back at all, Girlie?" he asked softly, after a while.

The schoolma'am shuddered eloquently in his arms.

"It was sure lonesome—it was *hell* out there alone," he observed, reminiscently.

"It was sure—h-hell back here alone, too," murmured a smothered voice which did not sound much like the clear, self-assertive tones of Miss Satterly.

"Well, it come near serving you right," Weary told her, relishfully grinning over the word she used.

"What made yuh chase me off?"

"I—don't know; I—"

"I guess yuh don't, all right," agreed Weary, giving a little squeeze by way of making quite sure he had her there.

"Say, what was that yarn Myrt Forsyth told yuh about me?"

"I—I don't know. She—she hinted a lot—"

"I expect she did—that's Myrt, every rattle uh the box," Weary cut in dryly.

"And she—she said you had to leave home—in the night—"

"Oh, she did, eh? Well, Girlie, if the time-table hasn't changed, Miss Myrt Forsyth sneaked off the same way. The train west leaves—or did leave—Chadville along about midnight, so—Say, it feels good to be back, little schoolma'am. You don't know how good—"

"I guess I do," cried the schoolma'am very emphatically. "I just guess I know something about that, myself. Oh you dear, great, tall—"

Something happened just then to the schoolma'am's lips, so that she could not finish the sentence.

FIRST AID TO CUPID

The floor manager had just called out that it was "ladies' choice," and Happy Jack, his eyes glued in rapturous apprehension upon the thin, expressionless face of Annie Pilgreen, backed diffidently into a corner. He hoped and he feared that she would discover him and lead him out to dance; she had done that once, at the Labor Day ball, and he had not slept soundly for several nights after. Someone laid proprietary hand upon his cinnamon-brown coat sleeve, and he jumped and blushed; it was only the schoolma'am, however, smiling up at him ingratiatingly in a manner wholly bewildering to a simple minded fellow like Happy Jack. She led him into another corner, plumped gracefully and with much decision down upon a bench, drew her skirts aside to make room for him and announced that she was tired and wanted a nice long talk with him. Happy Jack, sending a troubled glance after Annie, who was leading Joe Meeker out to dance, sighed a bit and sat down obediently—and thereby walked straight into the loop which the schoolma'am had spread for his unwary feet.

The schoolma'am was sitting out an astonishing number of dances—for a girl who could dance from dark to dawn and never turn a hair—and the women were wondering why. If she had sat them out with Weary Davidson they would have smiled knowingly and thought no more of it; but she did not. For every dance she had a different companion, and in every case it ended in that particular young man looking rather scared and unhappy. After five minutes of low-toned monologue on the part of the schoolma'am, Happy Jack went the way of his predecessors and also became scared and unhappy.

"Aw, say! Miss Satterly, *I* can't act," he protested in a panic.

"Oh, yes, you could," declared the schoolma'am, with sweet assurance, "if you only thought so."

"Aw, I couldn't get up before a crowd and say a piece, not if—"

"I'm not sure I want you to. There are other things to an entertainment besides reciting things. I only want you to promise that you will help me out. You will, won't you?" The schoolma'am's eyes, besides being pretty, were often disconcertingly direct in their gaze.

Happy Jack wriggled and looked toward the door, which suddenly seemed a very long way off. "I—I've got to go up to the Falls, along about Christmas," he stuttered feebly, avoiding her eyes. "I—I can't get off any other time, and I've—I've got a tooth—"

"You're the fifth Flying-U man who has 'a tooth,'" the schoolma'am interrupted impatiently. "A dentist ought to locate in Dry Lake; from what I have heard confidentially to-night, there's a fortune to be made off the teeth of the Happy Family alone."

Every drop of blood in Happy's body seemed to stand then in his face.

"I—I'll pull the curtain for yuh," he volunteered, meekly.

"You're the seventh applicant for that place." The schoolma'am was crushingly calm. "Every fellow I've spoken to has evinced a morbid craving for curtain-pulling."

Happy Jack crumpled under her sarcasm and perspired, and tried to think of something, with his brain quite paralyzed and useless.

The schoolma'am continued inexorably; plainly, *her* brain was not paralyzed. "I've promised the neighborhood that I would give a Christmas tree and entertainment—and when a school-teacher promises anything to a neighborhood, nothing short of death or smallpox will be accepted as an excuse for failing to keep the promise; and I've seven tongue-tied kids to work with!" (The schoolma'am was only spasmodically given to irreproachable English.) "Of course, I relied upon my friends to help me out. But when I come to calling the roll, I—I don't seem to *have* any friends." The schoolma'am was twirling the Montana sapphire ring which Weary had given her last spring, and her voice was trembly and made Happy Jack feel vaguely that he was a low-down cur and ought to be killed.

He swallowed twice. "Aw, yuh don't want to go and feel bad about it; I never meant—I'll do anything yuh ask me to."

"Thank you. I knew I could count upon you, Jack."

The schoolma'am recovered her spirits with a promptness that was suspicious; patted his arm and called him an awfully good fellow, which reduced Happy Jack to a state just this side imbecility. Also, she drew a little memorandum book from somewhere, and wrote Happy

Jack's name in clear, convincing characters that made him shiver. He saw other names above his own on the page; quite a lot of them; seven in fact. Miss Satterly, evidently, was not quite as destitute of friends as her voice, awhile back, would lead one to believe. Happy Jack wondered.

"I haven't quite decided what we will have," she remarked briskly. "When I do, we'll all meet some evening in the school-house and talk it over. There's lots of fun getting up an entertainment; you'll like it, once you get started." Happy did not agree with her, but he did not tell her so; he managed to contort his face into something resembling a grin, and retreated to the hotel, where he swallowed two glasses of whiskey to start his blood moving again, and then sat down and played poker disasterously until daylight made the lamps grow a sickly yellow and the air of the room seem suddenly stale and dead. But Happy never thought of blaming the schoolma'am for the eighteen dollars he lost.

Neither did he blame her for the nightmares which tormented his sleep during the week that followed or the vague uneasiness that filled his waking hour, even when he was not thinking directly of the ghost that dogged him. For wherever he went, or whatever he did, Happy Jack was conscious of the fact that his name was down on the schoolma'am's list and he was definitely committed to do anything she asked him to do, even to "speaking a piece"—which was in his eyes the acme of mental torture. When Cal Emmett, probably thinking of Miss Satterly's little book, pensively warbled in his ear:

Is your name written there,
On the page white and fair?

Happy Jack made no reply, though he suddenly felt chilly along the spinal column. It was.

"Schoolma'am wants us all to go over to the schoolhouse tonight—seven-thirty, sharp—to help make medicine over this Santa Claus round-up. Slim, she says you've got to be Santy and come down the stovepipe and give the kids fits and popcorn strung on a string. She says you've got the figure." Weary splashed into the wash basin like a startled muskrat.

The Happy Family looked at one another distressfully.

"By golly," Slim gulped, "you can just tell the schoolma'am to go plumb—" (Weary faced him suddenly, his brown hair running rivulets) "and ask the Old Man," finished Slim hurriedly. "He's fifteen pounds fatter'n I be."

"Go tell her yourself," said Weary, appeased. "I promised her you'd all be there on time, if I had to hog-tie the whole bunch and haul yuh over in the hayrack." He dried his face and hands leisurely and regarded the solemn group. "Oh, mamma! you're sure a nervy-looking bunch uh dogies. Yuh look like—"

"Maybe you'll hog-tie the whole bunch," Jack Bates observed irritably, "but if yuh do, you'll sure be late to meeting, sonny!"

The Happy Family laughed feeble acquiescence.

"I won't need to," Weary told them blandly. "You all gave the schoolma'am leave to put down your names, and its up to you to make good. If yuh haven't got nerve enough to stay in the game till the deck's shuffled yuh hadn't any right to buy a stack uh chips."

"Yeah—that's right," Cal Emmett admitted frankly, because shyness and Cal were strangers. "The Happy Family sure ought to put this thing through a-whirling. We'll give 'em vaudeville till their eyes water and their hands are plumb blistered applauding the show. Happy, you're it. You've got to do a toe dance."

Happy Jack grinned in sickly fashion and sought out his red necktie.

"Say, Weary," spoke up Jack Bates, "ain't there going to be any female girls in this opera troupe?"

"Sure. The Little Doctor's going to help run the thing, and Rena Jackson and Lea Adams are in it—and Annie Pilgreen. Her and Happy are down on the program for 'Under the Mistletoe', a tableau—the red fire, kiss-me-quick brand."

"Aw gwan!" cried Happy Jack, much distressed and not observing Weary's lowered eyelid.

His perturbed face and manner gave the Happy Family an idea. An idea, when entertained by the Happy Family, was a synonym for great mental agony on the part of the object of the thought, and great enjoyment on the part of the Family.

"That's right," Weary assured him sweetly, urged to further deceit by the manifest approval of his friends. "Annie's ready and willing to do her part, but she's afraid you haven't got the nerve to go through with it; but the schoolma'am says you'll have to anyhow, because your name's down and you told her distinct you'd do anything she asked yuh to. Annie likes yuh a heap, Happy; she said so. Only she don't like the way yuh hang back on the halter. She told me, private, that she wished yuh wasn't so bashful."

"Aw, gwan!" adjured Happy Jack again, because that was his only form of repartee.

"If I had a girl like Annie—"

"Aw, I never said I had a girl!"

"It wouldn't take me more than two minutes to convince her I wasn't as scared as I looked. You can gamble I'd go through with that living picture, and I'd sure kiss—"

"Aw, gwan! I ain't stampeding clear to salt water 'cause she said 'Boo!' at me—and I don't need no cayuse t' show me the trail to a girl's house—"

At this point, Weary succeeded in getting a strangle-hold and the discussion ended rather abruptly—as they had a way of doing in the Flying U bunk-house.

Over at the school-house that night, when Miss Satterly's little, gold watch told her it was seven-thirty, she came out of the corner where she had been whispering with the Little Doctor and faced a select, anxious-eyed audience. Even Weary was not as much at ease as he would have one believe, and for the others—they were limp and miserable.

She went straight at her subject. They all knew what they were there for, she told them, and her audience looked her unwinkingly in the eye. They did *not* know what they were there for, but they felt that they were prepared for the worst. Cal Emmett went mentally over the only "piece" he knew, which he thought he might be called upon to speak. It was the one beginning, according to Cal's version:

Twinkle, Twinkle little star,
What in thunder are you at?

There were thirteen verses, and it was not particularly adapted to a

Christmas entertainment.

The schoolma'am went on explaining. There would be tableaux, she said (whereat Happy Jack came near swallowing his tongue) and the Jarley Wax-works.

"What're them?" Slim, leaning awkwardly forward and blinking up at her, interrupted stolidly. Everyone took advantage of the break and breathed deeply.

The schoolma'am told them what were the Jarley Wax-works, and even reverted to Dickens and gave a vivid sketch of the original *Mrs. Jarley*. The audience finally understood that they would represent wax figures of noted characters, would stand still and let *Mrs. Jarley* talk about them—without the satisfaction of talking back—and that they would be wound up at the psychological moment, when they would be expected to go through a certain set of motions alleged to portray the last conscious acts of the characters they represented.

The schoolma'am sat down sidewise upon a desk, swung a neat little foot unconventionally and grew confidential, and the Happy Family knew they were in for it.

"Will Davidson" (which was Weary) "is the tallest fellow in the lot, so he must be the Japanese Dwarf and eat poisoned rice out of a chopping bowl, with a wooden spoon—the biggest we can find," she announced authoritatively, and they grinned at Weary.

"Mr. Bennett," (which was Chip) "you can assume a most murderous expression, so we'll allow you to be Captain Kidd and threaten to slay your Little Doctor with a wooden sword—if we can't get hold of a real one."

"Thanks," said Chip, with doubtful gratitude.

"Mr. Emmett, we'll ask you to be *Mrs. Jarley* and deliver the lectures."

When they heard that the Happy Family howled derision at Cal, who got red in the face in spite of himself. The worst was over. The victims scented fun in the thing and perked up, and the schoolma'am breathed relief, for she knew the crowd. Things would go with a swing, after this, and success was, barring accidents, a foregone conclusion.

Through all the clatter and cross-fire of jibes Happy Jack sat, nervous and distrait, in the seat nearest the door and farthest from Annie Pilgreen. The pot-bellied stove yawned red-mouthed at him, a scant three feet away. Someone coming in chilled with the nipping night air had shoveled in coal with lavish hand, so that the stove door had to be thrown open as the readiest method of keeping the stove from melting where it stood. Its body, swelling out corpulently below the iron belt, glowed red; and Happy Jack's wolf-skin overcoat was beginning to exhale a rank, animal odor. It never occurred to him that he might change his seat; he unbuttoned the coat absently and perspired.

He was waiting to see if the schoolma'am said anything about "Under the Mistletoe" with red fire—and Annie Pilgreen. If she did, Happy Jack meant to get out of the house with the least possible delay, for he knew well that no man might face the schoolma'am's direct gaze and refuse to do her bidding,

So far the Jarley Wax-works held the undivided attention of all save Happy Jack; to him there were other things more important. Even when he was informed that he must be the Chinese Giant and stand upon a coal-oil box for added height, arrayed in one of the big-flowered calico curtains which Annie Pilgreen said she could bring, he was apathetic. He would be required to swing his head slowly from side to side when wound up—very well, it looked easy enough. He would not have to say a word, and he supposed he might shut his eyes if he felt like it.

"As for the tableaux"—Happy Jack felt a prickling of the scalp and measured mentally the distance to the door—"We can arrange them later, for they will not require any rehearsing. The Wax-works we must get to work on as soon as possible. How often can you come and rehearse?"

"Every night and all day Sundays," Weary drawled.

Miss Satterly frowned him into good behavior and said twice a week would do.

Happy Jack slipped out and went home feeling like a reprieved criminal; he even tried to argue himself into the belief that Weary was only loading him and didn't mean a word he said. Still, the schoolma'am had said there would be tableaux, and it was a cinch she would tell Weary all about it—seeing they were engaged. Weary was the kind that found out things, anyway.

What worried Happy Jack most was trying to discover how the dickens Weary found out he liked Annie Pilgreen; that was a secret which Happy Jack had almost succeeded in keeping from himself, even. He would have bet money no one else suspected it—and yet here was Weary grinning and telling him he and Annie were cut out for a tableau together. Happy Jack pondered till he got a headache, and he did not come to any satisfactory conclusion with himself, even then.

The rest of the Happy Family stayed late at the school-house, and Weary and Chip discussed something enthusiastically in a corner with the Little Doctor and the schoolma'am. The Little Doctor said that something was a shame, and that it was mean, to tease a fellow as bashful as Happy Jack.

Weary urged that sometimes Cupid needed a helping hand, and that it would really be doing Happy a big favor, even if he didn't appreciate it at the time. So in the end the girls agreed and the thing was settled.

The Happy Family rode home in the crisp starlight gurgling and leaning over their saddle-horns in spasmodic fits of laughter. But when they trooped into the bunk-house they might have been deacons returning from prayer meeting so far as their decorous behavior was concerned. Happy

Jack was in bed, covered to his ears and he had his face to the wall. They cast covert glances at his carroty top-knot and went silently to bed—which was contrary to habit.

At the third rehearsal, just as the Chinese Giant stepped off the coal-oil box—thereby robbing himself miraculously of two feet of stature—the schoolma'am approached him with a look in her big eyes that set him shivering. When she laid a finger mysteriously upon his arm and drew him into the corner sacred to secret consultations, the forehead of Happy Jack resembled the outside of a stone water-jar in hot weather. He knew beforehand just about what she would say. It was the tableau that had tormented his sleep and made his days a misery for the last ten days—the tableau with red fire and Annie Pilgreen.

Miss Satterly told him that she had already spoken to Annie, and that Annie was willing if Happy Jack had no objections. Happy Jack had, but he could not bring himself to mention the fact.

The schoolma'am had not quoted Annie's reply verbatim, but that was mere detail. When she had asked Annie if she would take part in a tableau with Happy Jack, Annie had dropped her pale eyelids and said: "Yes, ma'am." Still it was as much as the schoolma'am, knowing Annie, could justly expect.

Annie Pilgreen was an anaemic sort of creature with pale eyes, ash-colored hair that clung damply to her head, and a colorless complexion; her conversational powers were limited to "Yes, sir" and "No, sir" (or Ma'am if sex demanded and Annie remembered in time). But Happy Jack loved her; and when a woman loves and is loved, her existence surely is justified for all time.

Happy Jack sent a despairing glance of appeal at the Happy Family; but the Family was very much engaged, down by the stove. Cal Emmett was fanning himself with *Mrs. Jarley's* poppy-loaded bonnet and refreshing his halting memory of the lecture with sundry promptings from Len Adams who held the book. Chip Bennett was whittling his sword into shape and Weary was drumming a tattoo in the great wooden bowl with the spoon he used to devour poisoned rice upon the stage. The others were variously engaged; not one of them appeared conscious of the fact that Happy Jack was facing the tragedy of his bashful life.

Before he realized it, Miss Satterly had somehow managed to worm from him a promise, and after that nothing mattered. The Wax-works, the tree, the whole entertainment dissolved into a blurred background, against which he was to stand with Annie Pilgreen, for the amusement of his neighbors, who would stamp their feet and shout derisive things at him. Very likely he would be subjected to the agony of an encore, and he knew, beyond all doubt, that he would never be permitted to forget the figure he should cut; for Happy Jack knew he was as unbeautiful as a hippopotamus and as awkward. He wondered why he, of all the fellows who were to take part, should be chosen for that tableau; it seemed to him they ought to pick out someone who was at least passably good-looking and hadn't such big, red hands and such immense feet. His plodding brain revolved the mystery slowly and persistently.

When he remounted his wooden pedestal, thereby transforming himself into a Chinese Giant of wax, he looked the part. Where the other statues broke into giggles, to the detriment of their mechanical perfection, or squirmed visibly when the broken alarm clock whirred its signal against the small of their backs, Happy Jack stood immovably upright, a gigantic figure with features inhumanly stolid. The schoolma'am pointed him out as an example to the others, and pronounced him enthusiastically the best actor in the lot.

"Happy's swallowed his medicine—that's what ails him," the Japanese

Dwarf whispered to Captain Kidd, and grinned.

The Captain turned his head and studied the brooding features of the giant. "He's doing some thinking," he decided. "When he gets the thing figured out, in six months or a year, and savvies it was a put-up job from the start, somebody'll have it coming."

"He can't pulverize the whole bunch, and he'll never wise up to who's the real sinner," Weary comforted himself.

"Don't you believe it. Happy doesn't think very often; when he does though, he can ring the bell—give him time enough."

"Here, you statues over there want to let up on the chin-whacking or I'll hand yuh a few with this," commanded *Mrs. Jarley*, and shook the stove-poker threateningly. The Japanese Dwarf returned to his poisoned rice and Captain Kidd apologized to his victim, who was frowning reproof at him, and the rehearsal proceeded haltingly.

That night, Weary rode home beside Happy Jack and tried to lift him out of the slough of despond. But Happy refused to budge, mentally, an inch. He rode humped in the saddle like a calf in its first blizzard, and he was discouragingly unresponsive; except once, when Weary reminded him that the tableau would need no rehearsing and that it would only last a minute, anyway, and wouldn't hurt. Whereupon Happy Jack straightened and eyed him meditatively and finally growled, "Aw gwan; I betche you put her up to it, yuh darned chump."

After that Weary galloped ahead and overtook the others and told them Happy Jack was thinking and mustn't be disturbed, and that he thought it would not be fatal to anyone, though it was kinda hard on Happy.

From that night till Christmas eve, Happy Jack continued to think. It was not, however, till the night of the entertainment, when he was riding gloomily alone on his way to the school-house, that Happy Jack really felt that his brain had struck pay dirt. He took off his hat, slapped his horse affectionately over the ears with it and grinned for the first time since the Thanksgiving dance. "Yes sir," he said emphatically aloud, "I betche that's how it is, all right and I betche—"

The schoolma'am, her cheeks becomingly pink from excitement, fluttered behind the curtain for a last, flurried survey of stage properties and actors. "Isn't Johnny here, yet?" she asked of Annie Pilgreen who had just come and still bore about her a whiff of frosty, night air. Johnny was first upon the program, with a ready-made address beginning, "Kind friends, we bid you welcome on this gladsome day," and the time for its delivery was overdue. Out beyond the curtain the Kind Friends were waxing impatient and the juvenile contingent was showing violent symptoms of descending prematurely upon the glittering little fir tree which stood in a corner next the stage. Back near the door, feet were scuffling audibly upon the bare floor and a suppressed whistle occasionally cut into the hum of subdued voices. Miss Satterly was growing nervous at the delay, and she repeated her question impatiently to Annie, who was staring at nothing very intently, as she had a fashion of doing.

"Yes, ma'am," she answered absently. Then, as an afterthought, "He's outside, talking to Happy Jack."

Annie was mistaken; Happy Jack was talking to Johnny. The schoolma'am tried to look through a frosted window. "I do wish they'd hurry in; it's getting late, and everybody's here and waiting." She looked at her watch. The suppressed whistle back near the door was gaining volume and insistence.

"Can't we turn her loose, Girlie?" Weary came up and laid a hand caressingly upon her shoulder.

"Johnny isn't here, yet, and he's to give the address of welcome. *Why* must people whistle and make a fuss like that, Will?"

"They're just mad because they aren't in the show," said Weary. "Say, can't we cut out the welcome and sail in anyway? I'm getting kinda shaky, dreading it."

The schoolma'am shook her head. It would not do to leave out Johnny—and besides, country entertainments demanded the usual Address of Welcome. It is never pleasant to trifle with an unwritten law like that. She looked again at her watch and waited; the audience, being perfectly helpless, waited also.

Weary, listening to the whistling and the shuffling of feet, felt a queer, qualmy feeling in the region of his diaphragm, and he yielded to a hunger for consolation and company in his misery. He edged over to where Chip and Cal were amusing themselves by peeping at the audience from behind the tree.

"Say, how do yuh stack up, Cal?" he whispered, forlornly.

"Pretty lucky," Cal told him inattentively, and the cheerfulness of his whole aspect grieved Weary sorely. But then, he explained to himself, Cal always did have the nerve of a mule.

Weary sighed and wondered what in thunder ailed him, anyway; he was uncertain whether he was sick, or just plain scared. "Feel all right, Chip?" he pursued; anxiously.

"Sure," said Chip, with characteristic brevity. "I wonder who those silver-mounted spurs are for, there on the tree? They've been put on since this afternoon—can't yuh stretch your neck enough to read the name, Cal? They're the real thing, all right."

Weary's dejection became more pronounced. "Oh, mamma! am I the only knock-kneed son-of-a-gun in this crowd?" he murmured, and turned disconsolately away. His spine was creepy cold with stage fright; he listened to the sounds beyond the shielding curtain and shivered. Just then Johnny and Happy Jack appeared looking rather red and guilty, and Johnny was thrust unceremoniously forward to welcome his kind friends and still the rising clamor.

Things went smoothly after that. It is true that Weary, as the Japanese Dwarf, halted the Wax-works and glared glassily at the faces staring back at him while the alarm clock buzzed unheeded against his spine. *Mrs. Jarley*, however, was equal to the emergency. She proceeded calmly to wind him up the second time, gave Weary an admonitory kick and whispered, "Come alive, yuh chump," and turned to the audience.

"This here Japanese Dwarf I got second-handed at a bargain sale for three-forty-nine, marked down for one week only," she explained blandly. "I got cheated like h— like I always do at them bargain sales, for it's about wore out. I guess I can make the thing work well enough to show yuh what it's meant to represent, though." She gave Weary another kick, commanded him again to "Come out of it and get busy," and the Dwarf obediently ate its allotted portion of poison. And every one applauded

Weary more enthusiastically than they had the others, for they thought it was all his part. So much for justice.

"Our last selection will be a tableau entitled, 'Under the Mistletoe,'" announced the schoolma'am's clear tones. Then she took up her guitar and went down from the stage to where the Little Doctor waited with her mandolin. While the tableau was being arranged they meant to play together in lieu of a regular orchestra. The schoolma'am's brow was smooth, for the entertainment had been a success so far; and the tableau would be all right, she was sure—for Weary had charge of that. She hoped that Happy Jack would not hate it so very much, and that it would help to break the ice between him and Annie Pilgreen. So she plucked the guitar strings tentatively and began to play.

Behind the curtain, Annie Pilgreen stood simpering in her place and Happy Jack went reluctantly forward, resigned and deplorably inefficient. Weary, himself again now that his torment was over, posed him cheerfully. But Happy Jack did not get the idea. He stood, as Weary told him disgustedly, looking like a hitching-post. Weary labored with him desperately, his ear strained to keep in touch with the music which would, at the proper time, die to a murmur which would be a signal for the red fire and the tableau. Already the lamps were being turned low, out there beyond the curtain.

Though it was primarily a scheme of torture for Happy Jack, Weary was anxious that it should be technically perfect. He became impatient. "Say, *don't* stand there like a kink-necked horse, Happy!" he implored under his breath. "Ain't there any joints in your arms?"

"I ain't never practised it," Happy Jack protested in a hoarse whisper. "I never even seen a tableau in my life, even. If somebody'd show me once, so's I could get the hang of it—"

"Oh, mamma! you're a peach, all right. Here, give me that sage brush!

Now, watch. We haven't got all night to make medicine over it. See?

Yuh want to hold it over her head and kinda bend down, like yuh were

daring yourself to kiss—"

Happy Jack backed off to get the effect; incidentally, he took the curtain back with him; also incidentally—, Johnny dropped a match into the red fire, which glowed beautifully. Weary caught his breath, but he was game and never moved any eyelash.

The red glow faded and left an abominable smell behind it, and some merciful hand drew the curtain—but it was not the hand of Happy Jack. He had gone out through the window and was crouching beneath it drinking in greedily the hand-clapping and the stamping of feet and the whistling, with occasional shouts of mirth which he recognized as coming from the rest of the Happy Family. It all sounded very sweet to the great, red ears of Happy Jack.

When the clatter showed signs of abatement he stole away to where his horse was tied, his sorrel coat gleaming with frost sparkles in the moonlight. "It's you and me to hit the trail, Spider," he croaked to the horse, and with his bare hand scraped the frost from the saddle.

A tall figure crept up from behind and grappled with him. Spider danced away as far as the rope would permit and snorted, and two struggling forms squirmed away from his untrustworthy heels.

"Aw, leggo!" cried Happy Jack when he could breathe again.

"I won't. You've got to come back and square yourself with Annie. How do yuh reckon she's feeling at the trick yuh played on her, yuh lop-eared—"

Happy Jack jerked loose and stood grinning in the moonlight. "Aw, gwan. Annie knowed I was goin' to do it," he retorted, loftily. "Annie and me's engaged." He got into the saddle and rode off, shouting back taunts.

Weary stood bareheaded in the cold and stared after him blankly.

WHEN THE COOK FELL ILL

It was four o'clock, and there was consternation in the round-up camp of the Flying U; when one eats breakfast before dawn—July dawn at that—covers thirty miles of rough country before eleven o'clock dinner and as many more after, supper seems, for the time being, the most important thing in the life of a cowboy.

Men stood about in various dejected attitudes, their thumbs tucked inside their chap-belts, blank helplessness writ large upon their perturbed countenances—they were the aliens, hired but to make a full crew during round-up. Long-legged fellows with spurs a-jingle hurried in and out of the cook-tent, colliding often, shouting futile questions, commands and maledictions—they were the Happy Family: loyal, first and last to the Flying U, feeling a certain degree of proprietorship and a good deal of responsibility.

Happy Jack was fanning an incipient blaze in the sheet-iron stove with his hat, his face red and gloomy at the prospect of having to satisfy fifteen outdoor appetites with his amateur attempts at cooking. Behind the stove, writhing bulkily upon a hastily unrolled bed, lay Patsy, groaning most pitiably.

"What the devil's the matter with that hot water?" Cal Emmett yelled at

Happy Jack from the bedside, where he was kneeling sympathetically.

Happy Jack removed his somber gaze from the licking tongue of flame which showed in the stove-front. "Fire ain't going good, yet," he said in a matter-of-fact tone which contrasted sharply with Cal's excitement.

"Teakettle's dry, too. I sent a man to the crick for a bucket uh water; he'll be back in a minute."

"Well, *move*! If it was you tied in a knot with cramp, yuh wouldn't take it so serene."

"Aw, gwan. I got troubles enough, cooking chuck for this here layout. I got to have some help—and lots of it. Patsy ain't got enough stuff cooked up to feed a jack-rabbit. Somebody's got to mosey in here and peel the spuds."

"That's your funeral," said Cal, unfeelingly.

Chip stuck his head under the lifted tent-flap. "Say, I can't find that cussed Three-H bottle," he complained. "What went with it, Cal?"

"Ask Slim; he had it last. Ain't Shorty here, yet?" Cal turned again to Patsy, whose outcries were not nice to listen to, "Stay with it, old-timer; we'll have something hot to pour down yuh in a minute."

Patsy replied, but pain made him incoherent. Cal caught the word "poison", and then "corn"; the rest of the sentence was merely a succession of groans.

The face of Cal lengthened perceptibly. He got up and went out to where the others were wrangling with Slim over the missing bottle of liniment.

"I guess the old boy's up against it good and plenty," he announced gravely. "He says he's poisoned; he says it was the corn."

"Well he had it coming to him," declared Jack Pates. "He's stuck that darned canned corn under our noses every meal since round-up started. He—"

"Oh, shut up," snarled Cal. "I guess it won't be so funny if he cashes in on the strength of it. I've known two or three fellows that was laid out cold with tin-can poison. It's sure fierce."

The Happy Family shifted uneasily before the impending tragedy, and their faces paled a little; for nearly every man of the range dreads ptomaine poisoning more than the bite of a rattler. One can kill a rattler, and one is always warned of its presence; but one never can tell what dire suffering may lurk beneath the gay labels of canned goods. But since one must eat, and since canned vegetables are far and away better than no vegetables at all, the Happy Family ate and took their chance—only they did not eat canned corn, and they had discussed the matter profanely and often with Patsy.

Patsy was a slave of precedent. Many seasons had he cooked beneath a round-up tent, and never had he stocked the mess-wagon for a long trip and left canned corn off the list. It was good to his palate and it was easy to prepare, and no argument could wean him from imperturbably opening can after can, eating plentifully of it himself and throwing the rest to feed the gophers.

"Ain't there anything to give him?" asked Jack, relenting. "That

Three-H would fix him up all right—"

"Dig it up, then," snapped Cal. "There's sure something got to be done, or we'll have a dead cook on our hands."

"Not even a drop uh whisky in camp!" mourned Weary. "Slim, you ought to be killed for getting away with that liniment."

Slim was too downhearted to resent the tone. "By golly, I can't think what I done with it after I used it on Banjo. Seems like I stood it on that rock—"

"Oh, hell!" snorted Cal. "That's forty miles back."

"Say, it's sure a fright!" sympathized Jack Bates as a muffled shriek came through the cloth wall of the tent. "What's good for tincaneetis, I wonder?"

"A rattling good doctor," retorted Chip, throwing things recklessly about, still searching. "There goes the damn butter—pick it up, Cal."

"If old Dock was sober, he could do something," suggested Weary. "I guess I'd better go after him; what do yuh think?"

"He could send out some stuff—if he was sober enough; he's sure wise on medicine."

Weary made him a cigarette. "Well, it's me for Dry Lake," he said, crisply. "I reckon Patsy can hang on till I get back; can poison doesn't do the business inside several hours, and he hasn't been sick long. He was all right when Happy Jack hit camp about two o'clock. I'll be back by dark—I'll ride Glory." He swung up on the nearest horse, which happened to be Chip's and raced out to the saddle bunch a quarter of a mile away. The Happy Family watched him go and called after him, urging him unnecessarily to speed.

Weary did not waste time having the bunch corralled but rode in among the horses, his rope down and ready for business. Glory stared curiously, tossed his crimpled, silver mane, dodged a second too late and found himself caught.

It was unusual, this interruption just when he was busy cropping sweet grasses and taking his ease, but he supposed there was some good reason for it; at any rate he submitted quietly to being saddled and merely nipped Weary's shoulder once and struck out twice with an ivory-white, daintily rounded hoof—and Weary was grateful for the docile mood he showed.

He mounted hurriedly without a word of praise or condemnation, and his silence was to Glory more unusual than being roped and saddled on the range. He seemed to understand that the stress was great, and fairly bolted up the long, western slope of the creek bottom straight toward the slant of the sun.

For two miles he kept the pace unbroken, though the way was not of the smoothest and there was no trail to follow. Straight away to the west, with fifteen miles of hills and coulees between, lay Dry Lake; and in Dry Lake lived the one man in the country who might save Patsy.

"Old Dock" was a land-mark among old-timers. The oldest pioneer found Dock before him among the Indians and buffalo that ran riot over the wind-brushed prairie where now the nation's beef feeds quietly. Why he was there no man could tell; he was a fresh-faced young Frenchman with much knowledge of medicine and many theories, and a reticence un-French. From the Indians he learned to use strange herbs that healed almost magically the ills of man; from the rough out-croppings of civilization he learned to swallow vile whiskey in great gulps, and to thirst always for more.

So he grew old while the West was yet young, until Dry Lake, which grew up around him, could not remember him as any but a white-bearded, stooped, shuffling old man who spoke a queer jargon and was always just getting drunk or sober. When he was sober his medicines never failed to cure; when he was drunk he could not be induced to prescribe, so that men trusted his wisdom at all times and tolerated his infirmities, and looked upon him with amused proprietorship.

When Weary galloped up the trail which, because a few habitations are strewn with fine contempt of regularity upon either side, is called by courtesy a street, his eyes sought impatiently for the familiar, patriarchal figure of Old Dock. He felt that minutes were worth much and that if he would save Patsy he must cut out all superfluities, so he resolutely declined to remember that cold, foamy beer refreshes one amazingly after a long, hot ride in the dust and the wind.

Upon the porch of Rusty Brown's place men were gathered, and it was evident even at a distance that they were mightily amused. Weary headed for the spot and stopped beside the hitching pole. Old Dock stood in the center of the group and his bent old figure was trembling with rage. With both hands he waved aloft his coat, on which was plastered a sheet of "tangle-foot" fly-paper. "Das wass de mean treeck!" he was shouting. "I don'd do de harm wis no mans. I tend mine business, I buy me mine clothes. De mans wass do dees treeck, he buy me new clothes—you bet you! Dass wass de mean—"

"Say, Dock," broke in Weary, towering over him, "you dig up some dope for tin-can poison, and do it quick. Patsy's took bad."

Old Dock looked up at him and shook his shaggy, white beard. "Das wass de mean treeck," he repeated, waving the coat at Weary. "You see dass? Mine coat, she ruint; dass was new coat!"

"All right—I'll take your word for it, Dock. Tell me what's good for tin—"

"Aw, I knows you fellers. You t'inke Ole Dock, she Dock, she don'd know nothings! You t'ink—"

Weary sighed and turned to the crowd. "Which end of a jag is this?" he wanted to know. "I've got to get some uh that dope-wisdom out uh him, somehow. Patsy's a goner, sure, if I don't connect with some medicine."

The men crowded close and asked questions which Weary felt bound to answer; everyone knew Patsy, who was almost as much a part of Dry Lake scenery as was Old Dock, and it was gratifying to a Flying-U man to see the sympathy in their faces. But Patsy needed something more potent than sympathy, and the minutes were passing.

Old Dock still discoursed whimperingly upon the subject of his ruined coat and the meanness of mankind, and there was no weaning his interest for a moment, try as Weary would. And fifteen miles away in a picturesque creek-bottom a man lay dying in great pain for want of one little part of the wisdom stored uselessly away in the brain of this drunken, doddering old man.

Weary's gloved hand dropped in despair from Old Dock's bent shoulder.

"Damn a drunkard!" he said bitterly, and got into the saddle. "Rusty,

I'll want to borrow that calico cayuse uh yours. Have him saddled up

right away, will yuh? I'll be back in a little bit."

He jerked his hat down to his eyebrows and struck Glory with the quirt; but the trail he took was strange to Glory and he felt impelled to stop and argue—as only Glory could argue—with his master. Minutes passed tumultuously, with nothing accomplished save some weird hoof-prints in the sod. Eventually, however, Glory gave over trying to stand upon his head and his hind feet at one and the same instant, and permitted himself to be guided toward a certain tiny, low-eaved cabin in a meadow just over the hill from the town.

Weary was not by nature given to burglary, but he wrenched open the door of the cabin and went in with not a whisper of conscience to say him nay. It was close and ill-smelling and very dirty inside, but after the first whiff Weary did not notice it. He went over and stopped before a little, old-fashioned chest; it was padlocked, so he left that as a last resort and searched elsewhere for what he wanted—medicine. Under the bed he found a flat, black case, such as old-fashioned doctors carried. He drew it out and examined if critically. This, also, was locked, but he shook it tentatively and heard the faintest possible jingle inside.

"Bottles," he said briefly, and grinned satisfaction. Something brushed against his hat and he looked up into a very dusty bunch of herbs. "You too," he told them, breaking the string with one yank. "For all I know, yuh might stand ace-high in this game. Lord! if I could trade brains with the old devil, just for to-night!"

He took a last look around, decided that he had found all he wanted, and went out and pulled the door shut. Then he tied the black medicine case to the saddle in a way that would give it the least jar, stuffed the bunch of dried herbs into his pocket and mounted for the homeward race. As he did so the sun threw a red beam into his eyes as though reminding him of the passing hours, and ducked behind the ridge which bounds Lonesome Prairie on the east.

The afterglow filled sky and earth with a soft, departing radiance when he stopped again in front of the saloon. Old Doc was still gesticulating wildly, and the sheet of fly-paper still clung to the back of his coat. The crowd had thinned somewhat and displayed less interest; otherwise the situation had not changed, except that a pinto pony stood meekly, with head drooping, at the hitching-pole.

"There's your horse," Rusty Brown called to Weary. "Yours played out?"

"Not on your life," Weary denied proudly. "When yuh see Glory played out, you'll see him with four feet in the air."

"I seen him that way half an hour ago, all right," bantered Bert Rogers.

Weary passed over the joke. "Mamma! Has it been that long?" he cried uneasily. "I've got to be moving some. Here, Dock, you put on that coat—and never mind the label; it's got to go—and so have you."

"Aw, he's no good to yuh, Weary," they protested. "He's too drunk to tell chloroform from dried apricots."

"That'll be all right," Weary assured them confidently. "I guess he'll be some sober by the time we hit camp. I went and dug up his dope-box, so he can get right to work when he arrives. Send him out here."

"Say, he can't never top off Powderface, Weary. I thought yuh was going to ride him yourself. It's plumb wicked to put that old centurion on him. He wouldn't be able to stay with him a mile."

"That's a heap farther than he could get with Glory," said Weary, unmoved. "Yuh don't seem to realize that Patsy's just next thing to a dead man, and Dock has got the name of what'll cure him sloshing around amongst all that whiskey in his head. I can't wait for him to sober up—I'm just plumb obliged to take him along, jag and all. Come on, Dock; this is a lovely evening for a ride."

Dock objected emphatically with head, arms, legs and much mixed dialect. But Weary climbed down and, with the help of Bert Rogers, carried him bodily and lifted him into the saddle. When the pinto began to offer some objections, strong hands seized his bridle and held him angrily submissive.

"He'll tumble off, sure as yuh live," predicted Bert; but Weary never did things by halves; he shook his head and untied his coiled rope.

"By the Lord! I hate to see a man ride into town and pack off the only heirloom we got," complained Rusty Brown.

"Dock's been handed down from generation to Genesis, and there ain't hardly a scratch on him. If yuh don't bring him back in good order Weary Davidson, there'll be things doing."

Weary looked up from taking the last half-hitch around the saddle horn. "Yuh needn't worry," he said. "This medical monstrosity is more valuable to me than he is to you, right now. I'll handle him careful."

"Das wass de mean treeck!" cried Dock, for all the world like a parrot.

"It sure is, old boy," assented Weary cheerfully, and tied the pinto's bridle-reins into a hard knot at the end. With the reins in his hand he mounted Glory. "Your pinto'll lead, won't he?" he asked Rusty then. It was like Weary to take a thing for granted first, and ask questions about it afterward.

"Maybe he will—he never did, so far," grinned Rusty. "It's plumb insulting to a self-respecting cow-pony to make a pack-horse out uh him. I wouldn't be none surprised if yuh heard his views on the subjects before yuh git there."

"It's an honor to pack heirlooms," retorted Weary. "So-long, boys."

Old Dock made a last, futile effort to free himself and then settled down in the saddle and eyed the world sullenly from under frost-white eyebrows heavy as a military mustache. He did not at that time look particularly patriarchal; more nearly he resembled a humbled, entrapped Santa Claus.

They started off quite tamely. The pinto leaned far back upon the bridle-reins and trotted with stiff, reluctant legs that did not promise speed; but still h went, and Weary drew a relieved breath. His arm was like to ache frightfully before they covered a quarter of the fifteen miles, but he did not mind that much; besides, he guessed shrewdly that the pinto would travel better once they were well out of town.

The soft, warm dusk of a July evening crept over the land and a few stars winked at them facetiously. Over by the reedy creek, frogs *cr-ek-ek-ekked* in a tuneless medley and night-hawks flapped silently through the still air, swooping suddenly with a queer, whooing rush like wind blowing through a cavern. Familiar sounds they were to Weary—so familiar that he scarce heard them; though he would have felt a vague, uneasy sense of something lost had they stilled unexpectedly. Out in the lane which leads to the open range-land between wide reaches of rank, blue-joint meadows, a new sound met them—the faint, insistent humming of millions of mosquitoes. Weary dug Glory with his spurs and came near having his arm jerked from its socket before he could pull him in again. He swore a little and swung round in the saddle.

"Can't yuh dig a little speed into that cayuse with your heels, Dock?" he cried to the resentful heirloom. "We're going to be naturally chewed up if we don't fan the breeze along here."

"Ah don'd care—das wass de mean treeck!" growled Dock into his beard.

Weary opened his mouth, came near swallowing a dozen mosquitoes alive, and closed it again. What would it profit him to argue with a drunken man? He slowed till the pinto, still moving with stiff, reluctant knees, came alongside, and struck him sharply with his quirt; the pinto sidled and Dock lurched over as far as Weary's rope would permit.

"Come along, then!" admonished Weary, under his breath. The pinto snorted and ran backward until Weary wished he had been content with the pace of a snail. Then the mosquitoes swooped down upon them in a cloud and Glory struck out, fighting and kicking viciously. Presently Weary found himself with part of the pinto's bridle-rein in his hand, and the memory of a pale object disappearing into the darkness ahead.

For the time being he was wholly occupied with his own horse; but when Glory was minded to go straight ahead instead of in a circle, he gave thought to his mission and thanked the Lord that Dock was headed in the right direction. He gave chase joyfully; for every mile covered in that fleet fashion meant an added chance for Patsy's life.

Even the mosquitoes found themselves hopelessly out of the race and beat up harmlessly in the rear. So he galloped steadily upon the homeward trail; and a new discomfort forced itself upon his consciousness—the discomfort of swift riding while a sharp-cornered medicine-case of generous proportions thumped regularly against his leg. At first he did not mind it so much, but after ten minutes of riding so, the thing grew monotonously painful and disquieting to the nerves.

Five miles from the town he sighted the pinto; it was just disappearing up a coulee which led nowhere—much less to camp. Weary's self-congratulatory mood changed to impatience; he followed after. Two miles, and he reached the unclimbable head of the coulee—and no pinto. He pulled up and gazed incredulously at the blank, sandstone walls; searched long for some hidden pathway to the top and gave it up.

He rode back slowly under the stars, a much disheartened Weary. He thought of Patsy's agony and gritted his teeth at his own impotence. After awhile he thought of Old Dock lashed to the pinto's saddle, and his conscience awoke and badgered him unmercifully for the thing he had done and the risk he had taken with one man's life that he might save the life of another.

Down near the mouth of the coulee he came upon a cattle trail winding up toward the stars. For the lack of a better clue he turned into it and urged Glory faster than was wise if he would save the strength of his horse; but Glory was game as long as he could stand, and took the hill at a lope with never a protest against the pace.

Up on the top the prairie stretched mysteriously away to the sky-line, with no sound to mar the broody silence, and with never a movement to disturb the deep sleep of the grass-land. All day had the hills been buffeted by a sweeping West wind; but the breeze had dropped with the sun, as though tired with roistering and slept without so much as a dream-puff to shake the dew from the grasses. Weary stopped to wind his horse and to listen, but not a hoof-beat came to guide him in his search. He leaned and shifted the medicine case a bit to ease his bruised leg, and wished he might unlock the healing mysteries and the magic stored within. It seemed to him a cruel world and unjust that knowledge must be gleaned slowly, laboriously, while men died miserably for want of it. Worse, that men who had gleaned should be permitted to smother such precious knowledge in the stupefying fumes of whiskey.

If he could only have appropriated Dock's brain along with his medicines, he might have been in camp by now, ministering to Patsy before it was too late to do anything. Without a doubt the boys were scanning anxiously the ridge, confident that he would not fail them though impatient for his coming. And here he sat helplessly upon a hilltop under the stars, many miles from camp, with much medicine just under his knee and a pocket crammed with an unknown, healing herb, as useless after all his effort as he had been in camp when they could not find the Three-H liniment.

Glory turned his head and regarded him gravely out of eyes near human in their questioning, and Weary laid caressing hand upon his silvery mane, grateful for the sense of companionship which it gave.

"You're sure a wise little nag." he said wistfully, and his voice sounded strange in the great silence. "Maybe you can find 'em—and it you can, I'll sure be grateful; you can paw the stars out uh high heaven and I won't take my quirt off my saddle-horn; hope I may die if I do!"

Glory stamped one white hoof and pointed both ears straight forward, threw up his head and whinnied a shrill question into the night. Weary hopefully urged him with his knees. Glory challenged once again and struck out eagerly, galloping lightly in spite of the miles he had covered. Far back on the bench-land came faint answer to his call, and Weary laughed from sheer relief. By the stars the night was yet young, and he grew hopeful—almost complacent.

Glory planted both forefeet deep in the prairie sod and skidded on the brink of a deep cut-bank. It was a close shave, such as comes often to those who ride the range by night. Weary looked down into blackness and then across into gloom. The place was too deep and sheer to ride into, and too wide to jump; clearly, they must go around it.

Going around a gulley is not always the simple thing it sounds, especially when one is not sure as to the direction it takes. To find the head under such conditions requires time.

Weary thought he knew the place and turned north secure in the belief that the gulley ran south into the coulee he had that evening fruitlessly explored. As a matter of fact it opened into a coulee north of them, and in that direction it grew always deeper and more impassable even by daylight.

On a dark night, with only the stars to guide one and to accentuate the darkness, such a discovery brings with it confusion of locality. Weary drew up when he could go no farther without plunging headlong into blackness, and mentally sketched a map of that particular portion of the globe and tried to find in it a place where the gulch might consistently lie. After a minute he gave over the attempt and admitted to himself that, according to his mental map, it could not consistently lie anywhere at all. Even Glory seemed to have lost interest in the quest and stood listlessly with his head down. His attitude irritated Weary very much.

"Yuh damn', taffy colored cayuse!" he said fretfully. "This is as much your funeral as mine—seeing yuh started out all so brisk to find that pinto. Do yah suppose yuh could find a horse if he was staked ten feet in front of your nose? Chances are, yuh couldn't. I reckon you'd have trouble finding your way around the little pasture at the ranch—unless the sun shone real bright and yuh had somebody to lead yuh!"

This was manifestly unjust and it was not like Weary; but this night's mission was getting on his nerves. He leaned and shifted the medicine-case again, and felt ruefully of his bruised leg. That also was getting upon his nerves. "Oh, Mamma!" he muttered disgustedly. "This is sure a sarcastic layout; dope enough here to cure all the sickness in Montana—if a fellow knew enough to use it—battering a hole in my leg you could throw a yearling calf into, and me wandering wild over the hills like a locoed sheepherder! Glory, you get a move on yuh, you knock-kneed, buzzard-headed—" He subsided into incoherent grumbling and rode back whence he came, up the gully's brim.

When the night was far gone and the slant of the Great Dipper told him that day-dawn was near, he heard a horse nicker wistfully, away to the right. Wheeling sharply, his spurs raking the roughened sides of Glory, he rode recklessly toward the sound, not daring to hope that it might be the pinto and yet holding his mind back from despair.

When he was near the place—so near that he could see a dim, formless shape outlined against the sky-line,—Glory stumbled over a sunken rock and fell heavily upon his knees. When he picked himself up he hobbled and Weary cursed him unpityingly.

When, limping painfully, Glory came up with the object, the heart of Weary rose up and stuck in his throat; for the object was a pinto horse and above it bulked the squat figure of an irate old man.

"Hello, Dock," greeted Weary. "How do yuh stack up?"

"*Mon Dieu*, Weary Davitson, I feex yous plandy. What for do you dees t'ing? I not do de harrm wis you. I not got de mooney wort' all dees troubles what you makes. Dees horse, she lak for keel me also. She buck, en keeck, en roon—*mon Dieu*, I not like dees t'ing."

"Sober, by thunder!" ejaculated Weary in an ecstatic half-whisper. "Dock, you've got a chance to make a record for yourself to-night—if we ain't too late," he added bodefully. "Do yuh know where we're headed for?"

"I t'ink for de devil," retorted Old Dock peevishly.

"No sir, we aren't. We're going straight to camp, and you're going to save old Patsy—you like Patsy, you know; many's the time you've tanked up together and then fell on each other's necks and wept because the good old times won't come again. He got poisoned on canned corn; the Lord send he ain't too dead for you to cure him. Come on—we better hit the breeze. We've lost a heap uh time."

"I not like dees rope; she not comforte. I have ride de bad horse when you wass in cradle."

Weary got down and went over to him. "All right, I'll unwind yuh. When we started, yuh know, yuh couldn't uh rode a rocking chair. I was plumb obliged to tie yuh on. Think we'll be in time to help Patsy? He was taken sick about four o'clock."

Old Dock waited till he was untied and the remnant of bridle-rein was placed in his hand, before he answered ironically: "I not do de mageec, *mon cher* Weary. I mos' have de medicine or I can do nottings, I not wave de fingaire an' say de vord."

"That's all right—I've got the whole works. I broke into your shack and made a clean haul uh dope. And I want to tell yuh that for a doctor you've got blame poor ventilation to your house. But I found the medicine."

"Mon Dieu!" was the astonished comment, and after that they rode in silence and such haste as Glory's lameness would permit.

The first beams of the sun were touching redly the hilltops and the birds were singing from swaying weeds when they rode down the last slope into the valley where camped the Flying-U.

The night-hawk had driven the horses into the rope-corral and men were inside watching, with spread loop, for a chance to throw. Happy Jack, with the cook's apron tied tightly around his lank middle, stood despondently in the doorway of the mess-tent and said no word as they approached. In his silence—in his very presence there—Weary read disaster.

"I guess we're too late," he told Dock, in hushed tones; for the minute he hated the white-bearded old man whose drunkenness had cost the Flying-U so dear. He slipped wearily from the saddle and let the reins drop to the ground. Happy Jack still eyed them silently.

"Well?" asked Weary, when his nerves would bear no more.

"When I git sick," said Happy Jack, his voice heavy with reproach,

"I'll send you for help—if I want to die."

"Is he dead?" questioned Weary, in hopeless fashion.

"Well," said Happy Jack deliberately, "no, he ain't dead yet—but it's no thanks to you. Was it poker, or billiards? and who won?"

Weary looked at him dully a moment before he comprehended. He had not had any supper or any deep, and he had ridden many miles in the long hours he had been away. He walked, with a pronounced limp on the leg which had been next the medicine-case, to where Dock stood leaning shakily against the pinto.

"Maybe we're in time, after all," he said slowly. "Here's some kind uh dried stuff I got off the ceiling; I thought maybe yuh might need it—you're great on Indian weeds." He pulled a crumpled, faintly aromatic bundle of herbs from his pocket.

Dock took it and sniffed disgustedly, and dropped the herbs contemptuously to the ground. "Dat not wort' notting—she what you call—de—cat_neep_." He smiled sourly.

Weary cast a furtive glance at Happy Jack, and hoped he had not overheard. Catnip! Still, how could he be expected to know what the blamed stuff was? He untied the black medicine-case and brought it and put it at the feet of Old Dock. "Well, here's the joker, anyhow," he said. "It like to wore a hole clear through my leg, but I was careful and I don't believe any uh the bottles are busted."

Dock looked at it and sat heavily down upon a box. He looked at the case queerly, then lifted his shaggy head to gaze up at Weary. And behind the bleared gravity of his eyes was something very like a twinkle. "Dis, she not cure seek mans, neider. She—" He pressed a tiny spring which Weary had not discovered and laid the case open upon the ground. "You see?" he said plaintively. "She not good for Patsy—she tree-dossen can-openaire."

Weary stared blankly. Happy Jack came up, looked and doubled convulsively. Can-openers! Three dozen of them. Old Dock was explaining in his best English, and he was courteously refraining from the faintest smile.

"Dey de new, bettaire kind. I send for dem, I t'ink maybe I sell. I put her in de grip—so—I carry dem all togedder. My mediceen, she in de beeg ches'."

Weary had sat down and his head was dropped dejectedly into his hands. He had bungled the whole thing, after all.

"Well," he said apathetically. "The chest was locked; I never opened it."

Old Dock nodded his head gravely. "She lock," he assented, gently.

"She mooch mediceen—she wort' mooch mooney. De key, she in mine

pocket—" "Oh, I don't give a damn where the key is—now," flared

Weary. "I guess Patsy'll have to cash in; that's all."

"Aw, gwan!" cried Happy Jack. "A sheepman come along just after you left, and he had a quart uh whisky. We begged it off him and give Patsy a good bit jolt. That

eased him up some, and we give him another—and he got to hollerin' so loud for more uh the same, so we just set the bottle in easy reach and let him alone. He's in there now, drunk as a biled owl—the lazy old devil. I had to get supper and breakfast too—and looks like I'd have to cook dinner. Poison—hell! I betche he never had nothing but a plain old belly-ache!"

Weary got up and went to the mess-tent, lifted the flap and looked in upon Patsy lying on the flat of his back, snoring comfortably. He regarded him silently a moment, then looked over his shoulder to where Old Dock huddled over the three dozen can-openers.

"Oh, mamma!" he whispered, and poured himself a cup of coffee.

THE LAMB

When came the famine in stock-cars on the Montana Central, and the Flying U herd had grazed for two days within five miles of Dry Lake, waiting for the promised train of empties, Chip Bennett, lately promoted foreman, felt that he had trouble a-plenty. When, short-handed as he was, two of his cowboys went a-spreeing and a-leisuring in town, with their faces turned from honest toil and their hands manipulating pairs and flushes and face-cards, rather than good "grass" ropes, he was positive that his cup was dripping trouble all round the rim.

The delinquents were not "top hands," it is true. They—the Happy Family, of which Jim Whitmore was inordinately proud—would sooner forswear their country than the Flying U. But even two transients of very ordinary ability are missed when they suddenly vanish in shipping time, and Chip, feeling keenly his responsibilities, rode disgustedly into town to reclaim the recreants or pay them off and hire others in their places.

With his temper somewhat roughened by the agent's report that no cars were yet on the way, he clanked into Rusty Brown's place after his deserters. One was laid blissfully out in the little back room, breathing loudly, dead to the world and the exigencies of life; him Chip passed up with a snort of disgust. The other was sitting in a corner, with his hat balanced precariously over his left ear, gazing superciliously upon his fellows and, incidentally, winning everything in sight. He leered up at Chip and fingered ostentatiously his three stacks of blues.

"What'n thunder do I want to go t' camp for?" he demanded, in answer to Chip's suggestion. "Forty dollars a month following your trail don't look good t' me no more. I'm four hundred dollars t' the good sence last night, and takin' all comers. Good money's just fallin' my way. I don't guess I hanker after any more night guardin', thank ye."

"Suit yourself," said Chip coldly, and turned away. Argument was useless and never to his liking. The problem now was to find two men who could take their places, and that was not so easily solved. A golden-haired, pink-cheeked, blue-eyed young fellow in dainty silk negligee, gray trousers, and russet leather belt, with a panama hat and absurdly small tan shoes, followed him outside.

"If you're looking for men," he announced musically, "I'm open for engagements."

Chip looked down at him tolerantly. "Much obliged, but I'm not getting up a garden-party," he informed him politely, and took a step. He was not in the mood to find amusement in the situation.

The immaculate one showed some dimples that would have been distracting in the face of a woman. "And I ain't looking for a job leading cows to water," he retorted. "Yuh shouldn't judge a man by his clothes, old-timer."

"I don't—a man!" said Chip pointedly. "Run away and play. I'll tell you what, sonny, I'm not running a kindergarten. Every man I hire has got man's work to do. Wait till you're grown up; as it is, you'd last quick on round-up, and that's a fact."

"Oh! it is, eh? Say, did yuh ever hear uh old Eagle Creek Smith, of the Cross L, or Rowdy Vaughan, or a fellow up on Milk River they call Pink?"

"I'd tell a man!" Chip turned toward him again. "At least I've heard of Eagle Creek Smith, and of Pink—bronco-fighter, they say, and a little devil. Why?"

The immaculate one lifted his panama, ran his fingers through his curls, and smiled demurely. "Nothing in particular—only, I'm Pink!"

Chip stared frankly, and measured the slender figure from accurately dented hat-crown to tiny shoe-tips. "Well, yuh sure don't look it," he said bluntly, at length. "Why that elaborate disguise of respectability?"

Pink sat him down on an empty beer case in the shade of the saloon and daintily rolled a cigarette.

"Yuh see, it's like this," he began, in his soft voice. "When the Cross L moved their stock across the line Rowdy Vaughan had charge uh the outfit; and, seeing we're pretty good friends, uh course I went along. I hadn't been over there a month till I had occasion t' thump the daylights out uh one uh them bone-headed grangers that vitiates the atmosphere up there; and I put him all to the bad. So a bunch uh them gaudy buck-policemen rose up and fogged me back across the line; a man has sure got t' turn the other cheek up there, or languish in *ga*-ol."

Pink brought the last word out as if it did not taste good. "I hit for the home range, which is Upper Milk River. But it was cussed lonesome with all the old bunch gone; so I sold my outfit and quit cow-punching for good. I wonder if

118

the puncher lives that didn't sell his saddle and bed, and reform at least once in his checkered career!

"I had a fair-sized roll so I took the home trail back to Minnesota, and chewed on the fatted calf all last winter and this summer. It wasn't bad, only the girls run in bunches and are dead anxious to tie up to some male human. I dubbed around and dodged the loop long as I could stand it, and then I drifted.

"I kinda got hungry for the feel of a good horse between m' legs once more. It made me mad to see houses on every decent bed-ground, and fences so thick yuh couldn't get out and fan the breeze if yuh tried. I tell yuh straight, old-timer, last month I was home I plumb wore out mother's clothes-line roping the gate-post. For the Lord's sake, stake me to a string! and I don't give a damn how rough a one it is!"

Chip sat down on a neighboring case and regarded the dapper little figure curiously. Such words, coming from those girlishly rosy lips, with the dimples dodging in and out of his pink cheeks, had an odd effect of unreality. But Pink plainly was in earnest. His eyes behind the dancing light of harmless deviltry, were pleading and wistful as a child.

"You're it!" said Chip relievedly. "You can go right to work. Seems you're the man I've been looking for, only I will say I didn't recognize yuh on sight. We've got a heap of work ahead, and only five decent men in the outfit. It's the Flying U; and these five have worked for the outfit for years."

"I sure savvy that bunch," Pink declared sweetly. "I've heard uh the

Happy Family before. Ain't you one uh them?"

Chip grinned reminiscently. "I was," he admitted, a shade of regret in his voice. "Maybe I am yet; only I went up a notch last spring. Got married, and settled down. I'm one of the firm now, so I had to reform and cut out the foolishness. Folks have got to calling the rest the Frivolous Five. They're a pretty nifty bunch, but you'll get on, all right, seeing you're not the pilgrim you look to be. If you were, I'd say: 'The Lord help you!' Got an outfit?"

"Sure. Bought one, brand new, in the Falls. It's over at the hotel now, with a haughty, buckskin-colored suitcase that fair squeals with style and newness." Pink pulled his silver belt-buckle straight and patted his pink-and-blue tie approvingly.

"Well, if you're ready, I'll get the horses these two hoboes rode in, and we'll drift. By the way, how shall I write you on the book?"

Pink stooped and with his handkerchief carefully, wiped the last speck of Dry Lake dust from his shiny toes. "Yuh won't crawfish on me, if I tell yuh?" he inquired anxiously, standing up and adjusting his belt again.

"Of course not." Chip looked his surprise at the question.

"Well, it ain't *my* fault, but my lawful, legal name is Percival

Cadwallader Perkins."

"Wha-at?"

"Percival Cad-*wall*-ader Perkins. Shall I get yuh something to take with it?"

Chip, with his pencil poised in air, grinned sympathetically. "It's sure a heavy load to carry," he observed solemnly. "How do you spell that second shift?"

Pink told him, spelling the word slowly, syllable by syllable. "Ain't it fierce?" he wanted to know. "My mother must have sure been frivolous and light-minded when I was born. I'm the only boy she ever had, and there was two grandfathers that wanted a kid named after 'em; they sure make a hot combination. Yuh know what Cadwallader means, in the dictionary?"

"Lord, no!" said Chip, putting away his book.

"Battle arranger," Pink told him sadly. "Now, wouldn't that jostle yuh? It's true, too; it has sure arranged a lot uh battles for me. It caused me to lick about six kids a day, and to get licked by a dozen, when I went to school. So, seeing the name was mine, and I couldn't chuck it, I went and throwed in with an ex-pugilist and learned the trade thorough. Since then things come easier. Folks don't open up the subject more'n a dozen times before they take the hint. And this summer I fell in with a ju-jutsu sharp—a college-fed Jap that sure savvied things a white man never dreams except in nightmares. I set at his feet all summer learning wisdom. I ain't afraid now to wear my name on my hatband."

"Still, I wouldn't," said Chip dryly. "Hike over and get the haughty new war-bag, and we'll hit the sod. I've got to be in camp by dinner-time."

A mile out Pink looked down at his festal garments and smiled. "I expect I'll be pickings for your Happy Family when they see me in these war-togs," he remarked.

Chip turned and regarded him meditatively for a minute. "I was just wondering," he said slowly, "if the Happy Family wouldn't be pickings for *you*."

Pink dimpled wickedly and said nothing.

The Happy Family were at dinner when Chip and Pink rode up and dismounted by the bed-tent. Chip and Pink went over to where the others were sitting in various places and attitudes, and the Happy Family received them, not with the nudges and winks one might justly expect, but with decorous silence.

Chip got plate, knife, fork, and spoon and started for the stove.

"Help yourself to the tools, and then come over here and fill up," he invited Pink, over his shoulder. "We don't stand on ceremony here. May look queer to you at first, but you'll get used to it."

The Happy Family pricked up its ears and looked guardedly at one another. This wasn't a chance visitor, then; he was going to work!

Weary, sitting cross-legged in the shade of a wagon-wheel looked up at Pink, fumbling shyly among the knives and forks, and with deceitful innocence he whistled absently:

  Oh, tell me, pretty maiden,
  Are there any more at home like you?

Pink glanced at him quickly, then at the solemn faces of the others, and retreated hastily inside the tent, where was Chip; and every man of them knew the stranger had caught Weary's meaning. They smiled discreetly at their plates and said nothing.

Pink came out with heaped plate and brimming cup, and retired diffidently to the farthest bit of shade he could find, which brought him close to Cal Emmett. He sat down gingerly so as not to spill anything.

"Going to work for the outfit?" asked Cal politely.

"Yes, sir; the overseer gave me a position," answered Pink sweetly, in his soft treble. "I just came to town this morning. Is it very hard work?"

"Yeah, it sure is," said Cal plaintively, between bites. "What with taming wild broncos and trying to keep the cattle from stampeding, our shining hours are sure improved a lot. It's a hard, hard life." He sighed deeply and emptied his cup of coffee.

"I—I thought I'd like it," ventured Pink wistfully.

"It's dead safe to prognosticate yuh won't a little bit. None of us like it. I never saw a man with soul so vile that he did."

"Why don't you give it up, then, and get a position at something else?"

Pink's eyes looked wide and wistful over the rim of his cup.

"Can't. We're most of us escaped desperadoes with a price on our heads." Cal shook his own lugubriously. "We're safer here than we would be anywhere else. If a posse showed up, or we got wind of one coming, there's plenty uh horses and saddles to make a getaway. We'd just pick out a drifter and split the breeze. We can keep on the dodge a long time, working on round-up, and earn a little money at the same time, so when we do have to fly we won't be dead broke."

"Oh!" Pink looked properly impressed. "If it isn't too personal—er—is there a—that is, are you——"

"An outlaw?" Cal assisted. "I sure am—and then some. I'm wanted for perjury in South Dakota, manslaughter in Texas, and bigamy in Utah. I'm all bad."

"Oh, I hope not!" Pink looked distressed. "I'm very sorry," he added simply, "and I hope the posses won't chase you."

Cal shook his head very, very gravely. "You can't most always tell," he declared gloomily. "I expect I'll have an invite to a necktie-party some day."

"I've been to necktie-parties myself." Pink brightened visibly. "I don't like them; you always get the wrong girl."

"I don't like 'em, either," agreed Cal. "I'm always afraid the wrong necktie will be mine. Were you ever lynched?"

Pink moved uneasily. "I—I don't remember that I ever was," he answered guardedly.

"I was. My gang come along and cut me down just as I was about all in.

I was leading a gang——"

"Excuse me a minute," Pink interrupted hurriedly. "I think the overseer is motioning for me."

He hastened over to where Chip was standing alone, and asked if he should change his clothes and get ready to go to work.

Chip told him it wouldn't be a bad idea, and Pink, carrying his haughty suit-case and another bulky bundle, disappeared precipitately into the bed-tent.

"By golly!" spoke up Slim, "it looks good enough to eat."

"Where did yuh pluck that modest flower, Chip?" Jack Bates wanted to know.

Chip calmly sifted some tobacco in a paper. "I picked it in town," he

told them. "I hired it to punch cows, and its name is—wait a minute."

He put away the tobacco sack, got out his book, and turned the leaves.

"Its name is Percival Cadwallader Perkins."

"Oh, mamma! Percival Cadwolloper—what?" Weary looked utterly at sea.

"Perkins," supplied Chip.

"Percival—Cad-wolloper—Perkins," Weary mused aloud.

"Yuh want to double the guard to-night, Chip; that name'll sure stampede the bunch."

"He's sure a sweet young thing—mamma's precious lamb broke out uh the home corral!" said Jack Bates. "I'll bet yuh a tall, yellow-haired mamma with flowing widow's weeds'll be out here hunting him up inside a week. We got to be gentle with him, and not rub none uh the bloom uh innocence off his rosy cheek. Mamma had a little lamb, his cheeks were red and rosy. And everywhere that mamma went—er—everywhere—that mamma—went——"

"The lamb was sure to mosey," supplied Weary.

"By golly! yuh got that backward," Slim objected. "It ought uh be:

Everywhere the lambie went; his mamma was sure to mosey."

The reappearance of Pink cut short the discussion. Pink as he had looked before was pretty as a poster. Pink as he reappeared would have driven a matinee crowd wild with enthusiasm. On the stage he would be in danger of being Hobsonized; in the Flying U camp the Happy Family looked at him and drew a long breath. When his back was turned, they shaded their eyes ostentatiously from the blaze of his splendor.

He still wore his panama, and the dainty pink-and-white striped silk shirt, the gray trousers, and russet-leather belt with silver buckle. But around his neck, nestling under his rounded chin, was a gorgeous rose-pink silk handkerchief, of the hue that he always wore, and that had given him the nickname of "Pink."

His white hands were hidden in a pair of wonderful silk-embroidered buckskin gauntlets. His gray trousers were tucked into number four tan riding-boots, high as to heel—so high that they looked two sizes smaller—and gorgeous as to silk-stitched tops. A shiny, new pair of silver-mounted spurs jingled from his heels.

He smiled trustfully at Chip, and leaned, with the studiously graceful pose of the stage, against a hind wheel of the mess-wagon. Then he got papers and tobacco from a pocket of the silk shirt and began to roll a cigarette. Inwardly he hoped that the act would not give him away to the Happy Family, whom he felt in honor bound to deceive, and bewailed the smoke-hunger that drove him to take the risk.

The Happy Family, however, was unsuspicious. His pink-and-white prettiness, his clothes, and the baby innocence of his dimples and his long-lashed blue eyes branded him unequivocally in their eyes as the tenderest sort of tenderfoot.

"Get onto the way he rolls 'em—backward!" murmured Weary into Cal's ear.

"If there's anything I hate," Cal remarked irrelevantly to the crowd, "it's to see a girl chewing a tutti-frutti cud—or smoking a cigarette!"

Pink looked up from under his thick lashes and opened his lips to speak, then thought better of it. The jingling of the cavvy coming in cut short the incipient banter, and Pink turned and watched intently the corralling process. To him the jangling bells were sweetest music, for which ears and heart had hungered long, and which had come to him often in dreams. His blood tingled as might a lover's when his sweetheart approaches.

"Weary, you and Cal better relieve the boys on herd," Chip called. "I'll get you a horse, P—Perkins"—he had almost said "Pink"—"and you can go along. Then to-night you'll go on guard with Cal."

"Yes, sir," said Pink, with a docility that would have amazed any who knew him well, and followed Chip out to the corral, where Cal and Weary were already inside with their ropes, among the circling mass.

Chip led out a gentle little cow-pony that could almost day-herd without a rider of any sort, and Pink bridled him before the covertly watching crew. He did not do it as quickly as he might have done, for he "played to the gallery" and deliberately fumbled the buckle and pinned one ear of the pony down flat with the head-stall.

A new saddle, stiff and unbroken, is ever a vexation unto its proud owner, and its proper adjustment requires time and much language. Pink omitted the language, so that the process took longer than it would naturally have done; but Cal and Weary, upon their mounts, made cigarettes and waited, with an air of endurance, and gave Pink much advice. Then he got somehow into the saddle and flapped elbows beside them, looking like a gorgeous-hued canary with wings a-flutter.

Happy Jack, who had been standing herd disconsolately with two aliens, stared open-mouthed at Pink's approach and rode hastily to camp, fair bursting with questions and comments.

The herd, twelve hundred range-fattened steers, grazed quietly on a side hill half a mile or more from camp. Pink ran a quick, appraising eye over the bunch estimating correctly the number, and noting their splendid condition.

"Never saw so many cattle in one bunch before, did yuh?" queried Cal, misinterpreting the glance.

Pink shook his head vaguely. "Does one man own all those cows?" he wanted to know, with just the proper amount of incredulous wonder.

"Yeah—and then some. This ain't any herd at all; just a few that we're shipping to get 'em out uh the way uh the real herds."

"About how many do you think there are here?" asked Pink.

Cal turned his back upon his conscience and winked at Weary. "Oh, there's only nine thousand, seven hundred and twenty-one," he lied boldly. "Last bunch we gathered was fifty-one thousand six hundred and twenty-nine and a half. Er—the half," he explained hastily in answer to Pink's look of unbelief, "was a calf that we let in by mistake. I caught it, after we counted, and took it back to its mother."

"I should think," Pink ventured hesitatingly, "it would be hard to find its mother. I don't see how you could tell."

"Well," said Cal gravely, sliding sidewise in the saddle, "it's this way. A calf is always just like its mother, hair for hair. This calf had white hind feet, one white ear, and the deuce uh diamonds on its left side. All I had to do was ride the range till I found the cow that matched."

"Oh!" Pink looked thoughtful and convinced.

Weary, smiling to himself, rode off to take his station at the other side of the herd. Even the Happy Family must place duty a pace before pleasure, and Cal, much as he would liked to have continued the conversation, resisted temptation and started down along the nearest edge of the bunch. Pink showed inclination to follow.

"You stay where you're at, sonny," Cal told him, over his shoulder.

"What must I do?" Pink straightened his tie and set his panama more firmly on his yellow curls, for a brisk wind was blowing.

Cal's voice came back to him faintly: "Just dub around here and don't do a darn thing; and don't bother the cattle."

"Good advice, that," Pink commented amusedly. "Hits day-herding off to a T." He prepared for a lazy afternoon, and enjoyed every minute.

On his way back to camp at suppertime, Pink rode close to Cal and looked as if he had something on his mind. Cal and Weary exchanged glances.

"I'd like to ask," Pink began timidly, "how you fed that calf—before you found his mother. Didn't he get pretty hungry?"

"Why, I carried a bottle uh milk along," Cal lied fluently. "When the bottle went empty I'd catch a cow and milk it."

"Would it stand without being tied?"

"Sure. All range cows'll gentle right down, if yuh know the right way to approach 'em, and the words to say. That's a secret that we don't tell anybody that hasn't been a cowboy for a year, and rode fourteen broncos straight up. Sorry I can't tell yuh."

Pink went diplomatically back to the calf. "Did you carry it in your arms, or—"

"The calf? Sure. How else would I carry it?" Cal's big, baby-blue eyes matched Pink's for innocence. "I carried that bossy in my arms for three days," he declared solemnly, "before I found a cow with white hind feet, one white ear, and the deuce uh—er—clubs——"

"Diamonds" corrected Pink, drinking in each word greedily.

"That's it: diamonds, on its right hind—er—shoulders——"

"The calf's was on its left side," reminded Pink reproachfully. "I don't believe you found the right mother, after all!"

"Yeah, I sure did, all right," contended Cal earnestly. "I know, 'cause she was that grateful, when she seen me heave in sight over a hill a mile away, she come up on the gallop, a-bawling, and—er—licked my hand!"

That settled it, of course. Pink dismounted stiffly and walked painfully to the cook-tent. Ten months out of saddle—with a new, unbroken one to begin on again— told, even upon Pink, and made for extreme discomfort. When he had eaten, hungrily and in silence, responding to the mildly ironical sociability of his fellows with a brevity which only his soft voice saved from bruskness, he unrolled his new bed and lay down with not a thought for the part he was playing. He heard with absolute indifference Weary's remark outside, that "Cadwolloper's about all in; day-herding's too strenuous for him." The last that came to him, some one was chanting relishfully:

  Mamma had a precious lamby his cheeks were red and rosy;

  And when he rode the festive bronk, he tumbled on his nosey.

There was more; but Pink had gone to sleep, and so missed it.

At sundown he awoke and went out to saddle the night horse Chip had caught for him, and then went to bed again. When shaken gently for middle guard, he dressed sleepily, added a pair of white Angora chaps to his afternoon attire, and stumbled out into the murky moonlight.

Guided and coached by Cal, he took his station and began that monotonous round which had been a part of the life he loved best. Though stiff and sore from unaccustomed riding, Pink felt quite content to be where he was; to watch the quiet land and the peaceful, slumbering herd; with the drifting gray clouds above, and the moon swimming, head under, in their midst. Twice in a complete round he met Cal, going in opposite direction. At the second round Cal stopped him.

"How yuh coming?" he queried cheerfully.

"All right, thank you," said Pink.

"Yuh want to watch out for a lop-horned critter over on the other side," Cal went on, in confidential tone. "He keeps trying to sneak out uh the bunch. Don't let him get away; if he goes, take after him and fog him back."

"He won't get away from me, if I can help it," Pink promised, and Cal rode on, with Pink smiling maliciously after him.

As he neared the opposite side, a dim shape angled slowly out before him, moving aimlessly away from the sleeping herd. Pink followed. Farther they went, and faster. Into a little hollow went the "critter", and circled. Pink took down his rope, let loose a good ten feet of it, and spurred unexpectedly close to it.

Whack! The rope landed with precision on the bowed shoulders of Cal. "Yuh will try to fool your betters, will yuh?" Whack! "I guess I can point out a critter that won't stray out uh the bunch again fer a spell!" Whack!

Cal straightened, gasping astonishment, in the saddle, pulled up with a jerk, and got off, in unlovely mood.

"And I can point to a little mamma's lamb that won't take down his rope to his betters again, either!" he cried angrily. "Climb down and get your ears cuffed proper, yuh darned, pink little smart Aleck; or them shiny heels'll break your pretty neck. Thump me with a rope, will yuh?"

Pink got down. Immediately after, to use a slang term, they "mixed." Presently Cal, stretched the long length of him in the grass, with Pink sitting comfortably upon his middle, looked up at the dizzying swim of the moon, saw new and uncharted stars, and nearer, dimly revealed in the half-light, the self-satisfied, cherubic face of Pink.

He essayed to rise and continue the discussion, and discovered a quite surprising state of affairs. He could scarcely move: and the more he tried the more painful became Pink's diabolical hold of him. He blinked and puzzled over the mystery.

"Of all the bone-headed, feeble-minded sons-uh-guns it's ever been my duty and pleasure to reconstruct," announced Pink melodiously, "you sure take the sour-dough biscuit. You're a song that's been tried on the cattle and failed t' connect. You're the last wail of a coyote dying in the dim distance. For a man that's been lynched and cut down and waiting for another yank, you certainly—are—mild! You're the tamest thing that ever happened. A lady could handle yuh with safety and ease. You're a children's playmate. For a deep-dyed desperado that's wanted for manslaughter in Texas, perjury in South Dakota, and bigamy in Utah, you're the last feeble whisper of a summer breeze. *You* cuff my ears proper? Oh, my! and oh, fudge! It is to laugh!"

Cat, battered as to features and bewildered as to mind, blinked again and grinned feebly.

"Yuh try an old gag that I wore out on humans of your ilk in Wyoming," went on Pink, warming to the subject. "Yuh load me with stuff that would bring the heehaw from a sheep-herder. Yuh can't even lie consistent to a pilgrim. You're a story that's been told and forgotten, a canto that won't rhyme, blank verse with club feet. You're the last, horrible example of a declining race. You're extinct."

"Say"—Pink's fists kneaded energetically Cal's suffering diaphragm.—"are yuh—all—ba-a-d?"

"Oh, Lord! No. I'm dead gentle. Lemme up."

"D'yuh think that critter will quit the bunch ag'in to-night?"

"He ain't liable to," Cal assured him meekly. "Say, who the devil are yuh anyhow?"

"I'm Percival Cadwallader Perkins. Do yuh like that name? Do yuh think it drips sweetness and poetry, like a card uh honey?"

"*Ouch*! It—it's *swell*!"

"You're a dam' liar," declared Pink, getting up.
"Furthermore, yuh old chuckle-head, yuh ought t' know better than try t' run any ranikaboos on me. I've got your pedigree, right back to the Flood; and it's safe betting yuh got mine, and don't know it. Your best girl happens to be my cousin."
Cal scrambled slowly and painfully to his feet. "Then you're Milk
River Pink. I might uh guessed it," he sighed.
"I cannot tell a lie," Pink averred. "Only, plain Pink'll do for me.
Where d'yuh suppose the bunch is by this time?"
They mounted and rode back together. Cal was deeply thoughtful.
"Say," he said suddenly, just as they parted to ride their rounds, "the boys'll be tickled plumb to death. We've been wishing you'd blow in here ever since the Cross L quit the country."
Pink drew rein and looked back, resting one hand on the cantle. "My gentle friend," he warned, "yuh needn't break your neck spreading the glad tidings. Yuh better let them frivolous youths wise-up in their own playful way, same as you done."
"Sure," agreed Cal, passing his fingers gingerly over certain portions of his face. "I ain't a hog. I'm willing they should have some sport with yuh, too."
Next morning, when Cal appeared at breakfast with a slight limp and several inches of cuticle missing from his features, the Happy Family learned that his horse had

fallen down with him as he was turning a stray back into the herd.

Chip looked up quizzically and then hid a smile behind his coffee-cup.

It was Weary that afternoon on dayherd who indulged his mendacity for the benefit of Pink; and his remarks were but paving-stones for a scheme hatched overnight by the Happy Family.

Weary began by looking doleful and emptying his lungs in sighs deep and sorrowful. When Pink, rising obligingly to the bait, asked him if he felt bad. Weary only sighed the more. Then, growing confidential, he told how he had dreamed a dream the night before. With picturesque language, he detailed the horror of it. He was guilty of murder, he confessed, and the crime weighed heavily on his conscience.

"Not only that," he went on, "but I know that death is camping on my trail. That dream haunts me. I feel that my days are numbered in words uh one syllable. That dream'll come true; you see if it don't!"

"I—I wouldn't worry over just a bad dream, Mr. Weary," comforted Pink.

"But that ain't all. I woke up in a cold sweat, and went outside. And there in the clouds, perfect as life, I seen a posse uh men galloping up from the South. Down South," he explained sadly, "sleeps my victim—a white-headed, innocent old man. That posse is sure headed for me, Mr. Perkins."

"Still, it was only clouds."

"Wait till I tell yuh," persisted Weary, stubbornly refusing comfort. "When I got up this morning I put my boots on the wrong feet; that's a sure sign that your dream'll come true. At breakfast I upset the can uh salt; which is bad luck. Mr. Perkins, I'm a lost man."

Pink's eyes widened; he looked like a child listening to a story of goblins. "If I can help you, Mr. Weary, I will," he promised generously.

"Will yuh be my friend? Will yuh let me lean on yuh in my dark hours?"

Weary's voice shook with emotion.

Pink said that he would, and he seemed very sympathetic and anxious for Weary's safety. Several times during their shift Weary rode around to where Pink was sitting uneasily his horse, and spoke feelingly of his crime and the black trouble that loomed so closer and told Pink how much comfort it was to be able to talk confidentially with a friend.

When Pink went out that night to stand his shift, he found Weary at his side instead of Cal. Weary explained that Cal was feeling pretty bum on account of that fall he had got, and, as Weary couldn't sleep, anyway, he had offered to stand in Cal's place. Pink scented mischief.

This night the moon shone brightly at intervals, with patches of silvery clouds racing before the wind and chasing black splotches of shadows over the sleeping land. For all that, the cattle lay quiet, and the monotony of circling the herd was often broken by Weary and Pink with little talks, as they turned and rode together.

"Mr. Perkins, fate's a-crowding me close," said Weary gloomily, when an hour had gone by. "I feel as if—what's that?"

Voices raised in excited talk came faintly and fitfully on the wind.

Weary turned his horse, with a glance toward the cattle, and, beckoning

Pink to follow, rode out to the right.

"It's the posse!" he hissed. "They'll go to the herd so look for me. Mr. Perkins, the time has come to fly. If only I had a horse that could drift!"

Pink thought he caught the meaning. "Is—is mine any good, Mr. Weary?" he quavered. "If he is, you—you can have him. I—I'll stay and—and fool them as—long as I can."

"Perkins," said Weary solemnly, "you're sure all right! Let that posse think you're the man they want for half an hour, and I'm safe. I'll never forget yuh!"

He had not thought of changing horses, but the temptation mastered him. He was riding a little sorrel, Glory by name, that could beat even the Happy Family itself for unexpected deviltry. Yielding to Pink's persuasions, he changed mounts, clasped Pink's hand affectionately, and sped away just as the posse appeared over a rise, riding furiously.

Pink, playing his part, started toward them, then wheeled and sped away in the direction that would lead them off Weary's trail. That is, he sped for ten rods or so. After that he seemed to revolve on an axis, and there was an astonishing number of revolutions to the minute.

The stirrups were down in the dark somewhere below the farthest reach of Pink's toes—he never once located them. But Pink was not known all over Northern Montana as a "bronco-peeler" for nothing. He surprised Glory even more than that deceitful bit of horseflesh had surprised Pink. While his quirt swung methodically, he looked often over his shoulder for the posse, and wondered that it did not appear.

The posse, however, was at that moment having troubles of its own. Happy Jack, not having a night horse saddled, had borrowed one not remarkable for its sure-footedness. No sooner had they sighted their quarry than Jack's horse stepped in a hole and went head-long—which was bad enough. When he got up he planted a foot hastily on Jack's diaphragm and then bolted straight for the peacefully slumbering herd—which was worse.

With stirrup-straps snapping like pistol-shots, he tore down through the dreaming cattle, with none to stop him or say him nay. The herd did not wait for explanations; as the posse afterward said, it quit the earth, while they gathered around the fallen Jack and tried to discover if it was a doctor or coroner that was needed.

When Jack came up sputtering sand and profane words, there was no herd, no horse and no Pink anywhere in that portion of Chouteau County. Weary came back, laughing at the joke and fully expecting to see Pink a prisoner. When he saw how things stood, he said "Mamma mine!"

and headed for camp on a run. The others deployed to search the range for a beef-herd, strayed, and with no tag for its prompt delivery.

Weary crept into the bed-tent and got Chip by the shoulder. Chip sat up, instantly wide-awake. "What's the matter?" he demanded sharply.

"Chip, we—we've lost Cadwolloper!" Weary's voice was tragic.

"Hell!" snapped Chip, lying down again. "Don't let that worry yuh."

"And we've lost the herd, too," added Weary mildly.

Chip got up and stayed up, and some of his remarks, Weary afterward reported, were scandalous.

There was another scene at sunrise that the Happy Family voted scandalous—and that was when they rode into a little coulee and came upon the herd, quietly grazing, and Pink holding them, with each blue eye a volcano shooting wrath.

"Yuh knock-kneed bunch uh locoed sheep-herders!" he greeted spitefully, "if yuh think yuh can saw off on your foolery and hold this herd, I'll go and get something to eat. When I come to this outfit t' work, I naturally s'posed yuh was cow-punchers. Yuh ain't. Yuh couldn't hold a bunch uh sick lambs inside a high board corral with the gate shut and locked on the outside. When it comes t' cow-science, you're the limit. Yuh couldn't earn your board on a ten-acre farm in Maine, driving one milk-cow and a yearling calf t' pasture and back. You're a hot bunch uh rannies—I don't think! Up on Milk River they'd put bells on every dam' one uh yuh t' keep yuh from getting lost going from the mess-house t' the corral and back. And, Mr. Weary, next time yuh give a man a horse t' fall off from, for the Lord's sake don't put him on a gentle old skate that would be pickings for a two-year-old kid. I thought this here Glory'd give a man something to do, from all the yawping I've heard done about him. I heard uh him when I was on the Cross L; and I will say right now that he's the biggest disappointment I've met up with in many a long day. He's punk. Come and get him and let me have something alive. I'm weary uh trying to delude myself into thinking that this red image is a horse."

The Happy Family, huddled ten paces before him, stared. Pink slid out of the saddle and came forward, smiling, and dimpling. He held out a gloved hand to the first man he came to, which was Weary himself. "Are yuh happy to meet Milk River Pink?" he wanted to know.

The Happy Family, grinning sheepishly, crowded close to shake him by the hand.

THE SPIRIT OF THE RANGE

Cal Emmett straightened up with his gloved hand pressed tight against the small of his back, sighed "Hully Gee!" at the ache of his muscles and went over to the water bucket and poured a quart or so of cool, spring water down his parched throat. The sun blazed like a furnace with the blower on, though it was well over towards the west; the air was full of smoke, dust and strong animal odors, and the throaty bawling of many cattle close-held. For it was nearing the end of spring round-up, and many calves were learning, with great physical and mental distress, the feel of a hot iron properly applied. Cal shouted to the horse-wrangler that the well had gone dry—meaning the bucket—and went back to work.

"I betche we won't git through in time for no picnic," predicted Happy Jack gloomily, getting the proper hold on the hind leg of a three-months-old calf. "They's three hundred to decorate yet, if they's one; and it'll rain—"

"You're batty," Cal interrupted. "Uh course we'll get through—we've *got* to; what d'yuh suppose we've been tearing the bone out for the last three weeks for?"

Chip, with a foot braced against the calf's shoulder, ran a U on its ribs with artistic precision. Chip's Flying U's were the pride of the whole outfit; the Happy Family was willing at any time, to bet all you dare that Chip's brands never varied a quarter-inch in height, width or position. The Old Man and Shorty had been content to use a stamp, as prescribed by law; but Chip Bennett scorned so mechanical a device and went on imperturbably defying

142

the law with his running iron—and the Happy Family gloated over his independence and declared that they would sure deal a bunch of misery to the man that reported him. His Flying U's were better than a stamp, anyhow, they said, and it was a treat to watch the way he slid them on, just where they'd do the most good.

"I'm going home, after supper," he said, giving just the proper width to the last curve of the two-hundredth U he had made that afternoon. "I promised Dell I'd try and get home to-night, and drive over to the picnic early to-morrow. She's head push on the grub-pile, I believe, and wants to make sure there's enough to go around. There's about two hundred and fifty calves left. If you can't finish up to-night, it'll be your funeral."

"Well, I betche it'll rain before we git through—it always does, when you don't want it to," gloomed Happy, seizing another calf.

"If it does," called Weary, who was branding—with a stamp—not far away, "if it does, Happy, we'll pack the bossies into the cook-tent and make Patsy heat the irons in the stove. Don't yuh cry, little boy—we'll sure manage *somehow*."

"Aw yes—*you* wouldn't see nothing to worry about, not if yuh was being paid for it. They's a storm coming—any fool can see that; and she's sure going to come down in large chunks. We ain't got this amatoor hell for nothing! Yuh won't want to do no branding in the cook-tent, nor no place else. I betche—"

"Please," spoke up Pink, coiling afresh the rope thrown off a calf he had just dragged up to Cal and Happy Jack, "won't somebody lend me a handkerchief? I want to gag Happy; he's working his hoodoo on us again."

Happy Jack leered up at him, consciously immune—for there was no time for strife of a physical nature, and Happy knew it. Everyone was working his fastest.

"Hoodoo nothing! I guess maybe yuh can't see that bank uh thunderheads. I guess your sight's poor, straining your eyes towards the Fourth uh July ever since Christmas. If yuh think yuh can come Christian Science act on a storm, and bluff it down jest by sayin' it ain't there, you're away off. I ain't that big a fool; I—" he trailed into profane words, for the calf he was at that minute holding showed a strong inclination to plant a foot in Happy's stomach.

Cal Emmett glanced over his shoulder, grunted a comprehensive refutation of Happy Jack's fears and turned his whole attention to work. The branding proceeded steadily, with the hurry of skill that makes each motion count something done; for though not a man of them except Happy Jack would have admitted it, the Happy Family was anxious. With two hundred and fifty calves to be branded in the open before night, on the third day of July; with a blistering sun sapping the strength of them and a storm creeping blackly out of the southwest; with a picnic tugging their desires and twenty-five long prairie miles between them and the place appointed, one can scarce wonder that even Pink and Weary—born optimists, both of them—eyed the west

144

anxiously when they thought no one observed them. Under such circumstances, Happy Jack's pessimism came near being unbearable; what the Happy Family needed most was encouragement.

The smoke hung thicker in the parched air and stung more sharply their bloodshot, aching eyeballs. The dust settled smotheringly upon them, filled nostrils and lungs and roughened their patience into peevishness. A calf bolted from the herd, and a "hold-up" man pursued it vindictively, swearing by several things that he would break its blamed neck—only his wording was more vehement. A cinder got in Slim's eye and one would think, from his language, that such a thing was absolutely beyond the limit of man's endurance, and a blot upon civilization. Even Weary, the sweet-tempered, grew irritable and heaped maledictions on the head of the horse-wrangler because he was slow about bringing a fresh supply of water. Taken altogether, the Happy Family was not in its sunniest mood.

When Patsy shouted that supper was ready, they left their work reluctantly and tarried just long enough to swallow what food was nearest. For the branding was not yet finished, and the storm threatened more malignantly. Chip saddled Silver, his own particular "drifter," eyed the clouds appraisingly and swung into the saddle for a fifteen-mile ride to the home ranch and his wife, the Little Doctor. "You can make it, all right, if yuh half try," he encouraged. "It isn't going to cut loose before dark, if I know the signs. Better put your jaw in a sling, Happy—

you're liable to step on it. Cheer up! to-morrow's the Day we Celebrate in letters a foot high. Come early and stay late, and bring your appetites along. Fare-you-well, my brothers." He rode away in the long lope that eats up the miles with an ease astonishing to alien eyes, and the Happy Family rolled a cigarette apiece and went back to work rather more cheerful than they had been.

Pleasure, the pleasure of wearing good clothes, dancing light-footedly to good music and saying nice things that bring smiles to the faces of girls in frilly dresses and with brown, wind-tanned faces and eyes ashine, comes not often to the veterans of the "Sagebrush Cavalry." They were wont to count the weeks and the days, and at last the hours until such pleasure should come to them. They did not grudge the long circles, short sleeps and sweltering hours at the branding, which made such pleasures possible—only so they were not, at the last, cheated of their reward.

Every man of them—save Pink—had secret thoughts of some particular girl. And more than one girl, no doubt, would be watching, at the picnic, for a certain lot of white hats and sun-browned faces to dodge into sight over a hill, and looking for one face among the group; would be listening for a certain well-known, well-beloved chorus of shouts borne faintly from a distance—the clear-toned, care-naught whooping that heralded the coming of Jim Whitmore's Happy Family.

To-morrow they would be simply a crowd of clean-hearted, clean-limbed cowboys, with eyes sunny and untroubled as a child's, and laughs that were good to hear and whispered words that were sweet to dream over until the next meeting. (If you ask the girls of the range-land, and believe their verdict, cowboys make the very best and most piquant of lovers.) Tomorrow there would be no hint of the long hours in the saddle, or the aching muscles and the tired, smarting eyes. They might, if pressed, own that they burnt the earth getting there, but the details of that particular conflagration would be far, far behind them— forgotten; no one could guess, to-morrow, that they were ever hot or thirsty or tired, or worried over a threatening storm, or that they ever swore at one another ill-naturedly from the sheer strain of anxiety and muscle-ache.

By sundown, so great was their industry, the last calf had scampered, blatting resentment, to seek his mother in the herd. Slim kicked the embers of the branding fire apart and emptied the water-bucket over them with a satisfied grunt.

"By golly, I ain't mourning because brandin's about over," he said.

"I'm plumb tired uh the sight uh them blasted calves."

"And we got through ahead of the storm," Weary sweetly reminded Happy

Jack.

Happy looked moodily up at the muttering black mass nearly over their heads and said nothing; Happy never did have anything to say when his gloomy predictions were brought to naught.

"I'm going to get on the bed-ground without any red tape or argument, if yuh ask *me*," volunteered Cal Emmett, rubbing his aching arms. "We want to get an early start in the morning."

"Meaning sun-up, I suppose," fleered Pink, who had no especial, feminine reason for looking forward with longing. With Pink, it was pleasure in the aggregate that lured him; there would be horse racing after dinner, and a dance in the school-house at night, and a season of general hilarity over a collection of rockets and Roman candles. These things appealed more directly to the heart of Pink than did the feminine element; for he had yet to see the girl who could disturb the normal serenity of his mind or fill his dreams with visions beautiful. Also, there was one thing about these girls that did not please him; they were prone to regard him as a sweet, amusing little boy whose dimples they might kiss with perfect composure (though of course they never did). They seemed to be forever taking the "Isn't he cunning!" attitude, and refused to regard him seriously, or treat him with the respect they accorded to the rest of the Happy Family. Weary's schoolma'am had offended him deeply, at a dance the winter before, by patting him indulgently on the shoulder and telling him to "Run along and find you a partner." Such things rankled, and he knew that the girls knew it, and that it amused them very much. Worse, the Happy Family knew it, and it amused them even more than it amused the girls. For this reason Pink would much prefer to sleep luxuriously late and ride over to the picnic barely in time for dinner and the races afterward. He did not want too long a time with the girls.

"Sure, we'll start at sun-up," Cal answered gravely. "We've got to be there by ten o'clock, so as to help the girls cut the cake and round up all the ham sandwiches; haven't we, Weary?"

"I should smile to remark," Weary assented emphatically. "Sun-up sure sees us on the road, Cadwolloper—and yuh want to be sure and wear that new pink silk handkerchief, that matches the roses in your cheeks so nice. My schoolma'am's got a friend visiting her, and she's been hearing a lot about yuh. She's plumb wild to meet yuh. Chip drawed your picture and I sent it over in my last letter, and the little friend has gone plumb batty over your dimples (Chip drawed yuh with a sweet smile drifting, like a rose-leaf with the dew on it, across your countenance, and your hat pushed back so the curls would show) and it sure done the business for Little Friend. Schoolma'am says she's a good-looker, herself, and that Joe Meeker has took to parting his hair on the dead center and wearing a four-inch, celluloid collar week days. But he's all to the bad—she just looks at your picture and smiles sad and longing."

"I hate to see a man impose on friendship," murmured Pink. "I don't want to spoil your face till after the Fourth, though that ain't saying yuh don't deserve it. But I will say this: You're a liar—you ain't had a letter for more than six weeks."

"Got anything yuh want to bet on that?" Weary reached challengingly toward an inner pocket of his vest.

"Nit. I don't give a darn, anyway yuh look at it. I'm going to bed." Pink unrolled his "sooguns" in their accustomed corner next to Weary's bed and went straightway to sleep. Weary thumped his own battered pillow into some semblance of plumpness and gazed with suspicion at the thick fringe of curled lashes lying softly upon Pink's cheeks.

"If I was a girl," he said pensively to the others, "I'd sure be in love with Cadwolloper myself. He don't amount to nothing, but his face 'd cause me to lose my appetite and pine away like a wilted vi'let. It's straight, about that girl being stuck on his picture; I'd gamble she's counting the hours on her fingers, right now, till he'll stand before her. Schoolma'am says it'll be a plumb sin if he don't act pretty about it and let her love him." He eyed Pink sharply from the tail of his eye, but not a lash quivered; the breath came evenly and softly between Pink's half-closed lips— and if he heard there was nothing to betray the fact. Weary sighed and tried again. "And that ain't the worst of it, either. Mame Beckman has got an attack; she told Schoolma'am she could die for Pink and never bat an eye. She said she never knowed what true love was till she seen him. She says he looks just like the cherubs—all but the wings—that she's been working in red thread on some pillow shams. She was making 'em for her sister a present, but she can't give 'em up, now; she calls all the cherubs 'Pink,' and kisses 'em night and morning, regular." He paused and watched anxiously Pink's untroubled face. "I tell yuh, boys, it's awful to have the fatal gift uh beauty, like Cadwolloper's got. He means all right, but he sure trifles a lot with girls' affections—which ain't right. Mamma! don't he look sweet, laying there so innocent? I'm sure sorry for Mame, though." He eyed him sidelong. But Pink slept peacefully on, except that, after a half minute, he stirred slightly and muttered something about "drive that darned cow back." Then Weary gave up in despair and went to sleep. When the tent became silent, save for the heavy breathing of tired men. Pink's long lashes lifted a bit, and he grinned maliciously up at the cloth roof.

For obvious reasons he was the only one of the lot who heard with no misgivings the vicious swoop of the storm; so long as the tent-pegs held he didn't care how hard it rained. But the others who woke to the roar of wind and the crash of thunder and to the swish and beat of much falling water, turned uneasily in their beds and hoped that it would not last long. To be late in starting for that particular scene of merry-making which had held their desires for so long would be a calamity they could not reflect upon calmly.

At three o'clock Pink, from long habit, opened his eyes to the dull gray of early morning. The air in the tent was clammy and chill and filled with the audible breathing of a dozen sleeping men; overhead the canvas was dull yellow and sodden with the steady drip, drip, drop of rain. There would be no starting out at sunrise—and perhaps there would be no starting at all, he thought with lazy disappointment, and turned on his side for another nap.

His glance fell upon Weary's up-turned, slumber-blank face, and his memory reverted revengefully to the baiting of the night before. He would fix Weary for that, he told himself spitefully; mentally measured a perpendicular line from Weary's face to the roof, reached up and drew his finger firmly down along the canvas for a good ten inches—and if you don't know why, try it yourself some time in a tent with the rain pouring down upon the land. As if that were not enough he repeated the operation again and again, each time in a fresh place, until the rain came through beautifully all over the bed of Weary. Then he lay down, cuddled the blankets up to his ears, closed his eyes and composed himself to sleep, at peace with his conscience and the world—and it did not disturb his self-satisfaction when Weary presently awoke, moved sleepily away from one drip and directly under another, shifted again, swore a little in an undertone and at last was forced to take refuge under his tarpaulin. After that Pink went blissfully off to dreamland.

At four o'clock it still rained dismally—and the Happy Family, waking unhappily one after another, remembered that this was the Fourth that they had worked and waited for so long, "swore a prayer or two and slept again." At six the sun was shining, and Jack Bates, first realizing the blessed fact, called the others jubilantly.

Weary sat up and observed darkly that he wished he knew what son-of-a-gun got the tent to leaking over him, and eyed Pink suspiciously; but Pink only knuckled his eyes like a sleepy baby and asked if it rained in the night, and said he had been dead to the world. Happy Jack came blundering under the ban by asking Weary to remember that he *told* him it would rain. As he slept beside Weary, his guilt was certain and his punishment, Weary promised himself, would be sure.

Then they went out and faced the clean-washed prairie land, filled their lungs to the bottom with sweet, wine-like air, and asked one another why in the dickens the night-hawk wasn't on hand with the cavvy, so they could get ready to start.

At nine o'clock, had you wandered that way, you would have seen the

Happy Family—a clean-shaven, holiday-garbed, resplendent Happy

Family—roosting disconsolately wherever was a place clean enough to

sit, looking wistfully away to the skyline.

They should, by now, have been at the picnic, and every man of them realized the fact keenly. They were ready, but they were afoot; the nighthawk had not put in an appearance with the saddle bunch, and there was not a horse in camp that they might go in search of him. With no herd to hold, they had not deemed it necessary to keep up any horses, and they were bewailing the fact that they had not forseen such an emergency—though Happy Jack did assert that he had all along expected it.

"By golly, I'll strike out afoot and hunt him up, if he don't heave in sight mighty suddent," threatened Slim passionately, after a long, dismal silence. "By golly, he'll wisht I hadn't, too."

Cal looked up from studying pensively his patent leathers. "Go on, Slim, and round him up. This is sure getting hilarious—a fine way to spend the Fourth!"

"Maybe that festive bunch that held up the Lewistown Bank, day before yesterday, came along and laid the hawk away on the hillside so they could help themselves to fresh horses," hazarded Jack Bates, in the hope that Happy Jack would seize the opening to prophesy a new disaster.

"I betche that's what's happened, all right," said Happy, rising to the bait. "I betche yuh won't see no horses t'day—ner no night-hawk, neither."

The Happy Family looked at one another and grinned. "Who'll stir the lemonade and help pass the sandwiches?" asked Pink, sadly. "Who'll push, when the school-ma'am wants to swing? Or Len Adams? or—"

"Oh, saw off!" Weary implored. "We can think up troubles enough,

Cadwolloper, without any help from you."

"Well, I guess your troubles are about over, cully—I can hear 'em coming." Pink picked up his rope and started for the horse corral as the belated cavvy came jingling around the nose of the nearest hill. The Happy Family brightened perceptibly; after all, they could be at the picnic by noon—if they hurried. Their thoughts flew to the crowd—and to the girls in frilly dresses—under the pine trees in a certain canyon just where the Bear Paws reach lazily out to shake hands with the prairie land.

Up on the high level, with the sun hot against their right cheeks and a lazy breeze flipping neckerchief ends against their smiling lips, the world seemed very good, and a jolly place to live in, and there was no such thing as trouble anywhere. Even Happy Jack was betrayed into expecting much pleasure and no misfortune, and whistled while he rode.

Five miles slipped behind them easily—so easily that their horses perked ears and tugged hard against the bits. The next five were rougher, for they had left the trail and struck out across a rough bit of barrenness on a short cut to the ford in Sheep Coulee. All the little gullies and washouts were swept clean and smooth with the storm, and the grass roots showed white where the soil had washed away. They hoped the rain had not reached to the mountains and spoiled the picnic grounds, and wondered what time the girls would have dinner ready.

So they rode down the steep trail into Sheep Coulee, galloped a quarter mile and stopped, amazed, at the ford. The creek was running bank full; more, it was churning along like a mill-race, yellow with the clay it carried and necked with great patches of dirty foam.

"I guess here's where we don't cross," said Weary, whistling mild dismay.

"Now, wouldn't that jostle yuh?" asked Pink, of no one in particular.

"By golly, the lemonade 'll be cold, and so'll the san'wiches, before we git there," put in Slim, with one of his sporadic efforts to be funny. "We got t' go back."

"Back nothing," chorused five outraged voices. "We'll hunt some other crossing."

"Down the creek a piece—yuh mind where that old sandbar runs half across? We'll try that." Weary's tone was hopeful, and they turned and followed him.

Half a mile along the raging little creek they galloped, with no place where they dared to cross. Then, loping around a willow-fringed bend, Weary and Pink, who were ahead, drew their horses back upon their haunches. They had all but run over a huddle of humanity lying in the fringe of weeds and tall grasses that grew next the willows.

"What in thunder—" began Cal, pulling up. They slid off their horses and bent curiously over the figure. Weary turned it investigatively by a shoulder. The figure stirred, and groaned. "It's somebody hurt; take a hand here, and help carry him out where the sun shines. He's wet to the skin," commanded Weary sharply.

When they lifted him he opened his eyes and looked at them; while they carried him tenderly out from the wet tangle and into the warmth of the sun, he set his teeth against the groans that would come. They stood around him uneasily and looked down at him. He was young, like themselves, and he was a stranger; also, he was dressed like a cowboy, in chaps, high-heeled boots and silver-mounted spurs. The chaps were sodden and heavy with water, as was the rest of his clothing.

"He must uh laid out in all that storm, last night," observed Cal, in a subdued voice. "He—"

"Somebody better ride back and have the bed wagon brought up, so we can haul him to a doctor," suggested Pink. "He's hurt."

The stranger's eyes swept the faces of the Happy Family anxiously. "Not on your life," he protested weakly. "I don't want any doctor—in mine, thank yuh. I—it's no use, anyhow."

"The hell it ain't!" Pink was drawing off his coat to make a pillow.

"You're hurt, somehow, ain't yuh?"

"I'm—dying," the other said, laconically. "So yuh needn't go to any trouble, on my account. From the looks—yuh was headed for some—blowout. Go on, and let me be."

The Happy Family looked at one another incredulously; they were so likely to ride on!

"I guess you don't savvy this bunch, old-timer," said Weary calmly, speaking for the six. "We're going to do what we can. If yuh don't mind telling us where yuh got hurt—"

The lips of the other curled bitterly. "I was shot," he said distinctly, "by the sheriff and his bunch. But I got away. Last night I tried to cross the creek, and my horse went on down. It was storming—fierce. I got out, somehow, and crawled into the weeds. Laying out in the rain—didn't help me none. It's—all off."

"There ought to be *something*—" began Jack Bates helplessly.

157

"There is. If yuh'll just put me away—afterwards—and say nothing,—I'll be—mighty grateful." He was looking at them sharply, as if a great deal depended upon their answer.

The Happy Family was dazed. The very suddenness of this unlooked-for glimpse into the somber eyes of Tragedy was unnerving. The world had seemed such a jolly place; ten minutes ago—five minutes, even, their greatest fear had been getting to the picnic too late for dinner. And here was a man at their feet, calmly telling them that he was about to die, and asking only a hurried burial and a silence after. Happy Jack swallowed painfully and shifted his feet in the grass.

"Of course, if yuh'd feel better handing me over—"

"That'll be about enough on that subject," Pink interrupted with decision. "Just because yuh happen to be down and out—for the time being—is no reason why yuh should insult folks. You can take it for granted we'll do what we can for yuh; the question is, *what*? Yuh needn' go talking about cashing in—they's no sense in it. You'll be all right.—"

"Huh. You wait and see." The fellow's mouth set grimly upon another groan. "If you was shot through, and stuck to the saddle—and rode—and then got pummeled—by a creek at flood, and if yuh laid out in the rain—all night— Hell, boys! Yuh know I'm about all in. I'm hard to kill, or I'd have been—dead— What I want to know—will yuh do what I—said? Will yuh bury me—right here—and keep it— quiet?"

The Happy Family moved uncomfortably. They hated to see him lying that way, and talking in short, jerky sentences, and looking so ghastly, and yet so cool—as if dying were quite an everyday affair.

"I don't see why yuh ask us to do it," spoke Cal Emmet bluntly. "What we want to do is get yuh to help. The chances is you could be—cured. We—"

"Look here." The fellow raised himself painfully to an elbow, and fell back again. "I've got folks—and they don't know—about this scrape. They're square—and stand at the top—And they don't—it would just about— For God sake, boys! Can't yuh see—how I feel? Nobody knows— about this. The sheriff didn't know—they came up on me in the dusk—and I fought. I wouldn't be taken—And it's my first bad break—because I got in with a bad—lot. They'll know something—happened, when they find—my horse. But they'll think—it's just drowning, if they don't find—me with a bullet or two— Can't yuh *see*?"

The Happy Family looked away across the coulee, and there were eyes that saw little of the yellow sunlight lying soft on the green hillside beyond. The world was not a good place; it was a grim, pitiless place, and—a man was dying, at their very feet.

"But what about the rest oh the bunch?" croaked Happy Jack, true to his misanthropic nature, but exceeding husky as to voice. "They'll likely tell—"

The dying man shook his head eagerly. "They won't; they're both—dead. One was killed—last night. The other when we first tried—to make a getaway. It—it's up to you, boys."

Pink swallowed twice, and knelt beside him; the others remained standing, grouped like mourners around an open grave.

"Yuh needn't worry about us," Pink said softly, "You can count on us, old boy. If you're dead sure a doctor—"

"Drop it!" the other broke in harshly. "I don't want to live. And if I did, I couldn't. I ain't guessing—I know."

They said little, after that. The wounded man seemed apathetically waiting for the end, and not inclined to further speech. Since they had tacitly promised to do as he wished, he lay with eyes half closed, watching idly the clouds drifting across to the skyline, hardly moving.

The Happy Family sat listlessly around on convenient rocks, and watched the clouds also, and the yellow patches of foam racing down the muddy creek. Very quiet they were—so quiet that little, brown birds hopped close, and sang from swaying weeds almost within reach of them. The Happy Family listened dully to the songs, and waited. They did not even think to make a cigarette.

The sun climbed higher and shone hotly down upon them. The dying man blinked at the glare, and Happy Jack took off his hat and tilted it over the face of the other, and asked him if he wouldn't like to be moved into the shade.

"No matter—I'll be in the shade—soon enough," he returned quietly, and something gripped their throats to aching. His voice, they observed, was weaker than it had been.

Weary took a long breath, and moved closer. "I wish you'd let us get help," he said, wistfully. It all seemed so horribly brutal, their sitting around him like that, waiting passively for him to die.

"I know—yuh hate it. But it's—all yuh can do. It's all I want." He took his eyes from the drifting, white clouds, and looked from face to face. "You're the whitest bunch—I'd like to know—who yuh are. Maybe I can put in—a good word for yuh—on the new range—where I'm going. I'd sure like to do—something—"

"Then for the Lord's sake, don't say such things!" cried Pink, shakily. "You'll have us—so damn broke up—"

"All right—I won't. So long,—boys. See yuh later—"

"Mamma!" whispered Weary, and got up hastily and walked away. Slim followed him a few paces, then turned resolutely and went back. It seemed cowardly to leave the rest to bear it—and somebody had to. They were breathing quickly, and they were staring across the coulee with eyes that saw nothing; their lips were shut very tightly together. Weary came back and stood with his back turned. Pink moved a bit, glanced furtively at the long, quiet figure beside him, and dropped his face into his gloved hands.

Glory threw up his head, glanced across the coulee at a band of range horses trooping down a gully to drink at the river, and whinnied shrilly. The Happy Family started and awoke to the stern necessities of life. They stood up, and walked a little way from the spot, avoiding one another's eyes.

"Somebody'll have to go back to camp," said Cal Emmett, in the hushed tone that death ever compels from the living. "We've got to have a spade—"

"It better be the handiest liar, then," Jack Bates put in hastily.

"If that old loose-tongued Patsy ever gets next—"

"Weary better go—and Pink. They're the best liars in the bunch," said Cal, trying unsuccessfully to get back his everyday manner.

Pink and Weary went over and took the dragging bridle-reins of their mounts, caught a stirrup and swung up into the saddles silently.

"And say!" Happy Jack called softly, as they were going down the slope. "Yuh better bring—a blanket."

Weary nodded, and they rode away, their horses stepping softly in the thick grasses. When they were passed quite out of the presence of the dead, they spurred their horses into a gallop.

The sun marked mid-afternoon when they returned, and the four who had waited drew long breaths of relief at sight of them.

"We told Patsy we'd run onto a—den—"

"Oh, shut up, can't yuh?" Jack Bates interrupted shortly. "Yuh'll have plenty uh time to tell us afterwards."

"We've got a place picked out," said Cal, and led them a little distance up the slope, to a level spot in the shadow of a huge, gray bowlder. "That's his headstone," he said, soberly. "The poor devil won't be cheated out uh that, if we *can't* mark it with his name. It'll last as long as he'll need it."

Only in the West, perhaps, may one find a funeral like that. No minister stood at the head of the grave and read, "Dust to dust" and all the heartbreaking rest of it. There was no singing but from a meadowlark that perched on a nearby rock and rippled his brief song when, with their ropes, they lowered the blanket wrapped form. They stood, with bare heads bowed, while the meadow lark sang. When he had flown, Pink, looking a choir-boy in disguise, repeated softly and incorrectly the Lord's prayer. The Happy Family did not feel that there was any incongruity in what they did. When Pink, gulping a little over the unfamiliar words, said:

"Thine be power and glory—Amen;" five clear, youthful voices added the Amen quite simply. Then they filled the grave and stood silent a minute before they went down to where their horse stood waiting patiently, with now and then a curious glance up the hill to where their masters grouped.

The Happy Family mounted and without a backward glance rode soberly away; and the trail they took led, not to the picnic, but to camp.

THE REVELER

Happy Jack, coming from Dry Lake where he had been sent for the mail, rode up to the Flying U camp just at dinner time and dismounted gloomily and in silence. His horse looked fagged—which was unusual in Happy's mounts unless there was urgent need of haste or he was out with the rest of the Family and constrained to adopt their pace, which was rapid. Happy, when riding alone, loved best to hump forward over the horn and jog along slowly, half asleep.

"Something's hurting Happy," was Cal Emmett's verdict when he saw the condition of the horse.

"He's got a burden on his mind as big as a haystack," grinned Jack Bates. "Watch the way his jaw hangs down, will yuh? Bet yuh somebody's dead."

"Most likely it's something he thinks is *going* to happen," said Pink. "Happy always makes me think of a play I seen when I was back home; it starts out with a melancholy cuss coming out and giving a sigh that near lifts him off his feet, and he says: 'In *soo-ooth* I know not *why* I am so sa-ad.' That's Happy all over."

The Happy Family giggled and went on with their dinner, for Happy Jack was too close for further comments not intended for his ears. They waited demurely, but in secret mirth, for him to unburden his mind. They knew that they would not have long to wait; Happy, bird of ill omen that he was, enjoyed much the telling of bad news.

"Weary's in town," he announced heavily, coming over and getting himself a plate and cup.

The Happy Family were secretly a bit disappointed; this promised, after all, to be tame.

"Did he bring the horses?" asked Chip, glancing up over the brim of his cup.

"I dunno," Happy responded from the stove, where he was trying how much of everything he could possibly pile upon his plate without spilling anything. "I didn't see no horses—but the one he was ridin'."

Weary had been sent, two weeks ago, to the upper Marias country after three saddle horses that had strayed from the home range, and which had been seen near Shelby. It was quite time for him to return, if he expected to catch the Flying U wagon before it pulled out on the beef roundup. That he should be in town and not ride out with Happy Jack was a bit strange.

"Why don't yuh throw it out uh yuh, yuh big, long-jawed croaker?" demanded Pink in a voice queerly soft and girlish. It had been a real grievance to him that he had not been permitted to go with Weary, who was his particular chum. "What's the matter? Is Weary sick?"

"No," said Happy Jack deliberately, "I guess he ain't what yuh could call *sick*."

"Why didn't he come out with you, then?" asked Chip, sharply. Happy did get on one's nerves so.

"Well, I ast him t' come—and he took a shot at me for it." There was an instant's dead silence. Then Jack Bates laughed uneasily.

"Happy, how many horses did yuh ride out to camp?"

Happy Jack had, upon one occasion, looked too long upon the wine—or whisky, to be more explicit. Afterward, he had insisted that he was riding two horses home, instead of one. He was not permitted to forget that defection. The Happy Family had an unpleasant habit of recalling the incident whenever Happy Jack made a statement which they felt disinclined to credit—as this last statement was.

Happy Jack whirled on the speaker. "Aw, shut up! I never kidnaped no girl off'n no train, and—"

Jack Bates colored and got belligerently to his feet. That hit him in an exceedingly tender place.

"Happy, look here," Chip cut in authoritatively. "What's wrong with Weary? If he took a shot at you, it's a cinch he had some reason for it."

Weary was even dearer to the heart of Chip than to Pink. "Ah—he never! He's takin' shots permisc'us, lemme tell yuh. And he ain't troublin' about no *reason* fer what he's doin'. He's plumb oary-eyed—that's what. He's on a limb that beats any I ever seen. He's drunk—drunk as a boiled owl, and he don't give a damn. He's lost his hat, and he's swapped cayuses with somebody—a measly old bench— and he's shootin' up the town t' beat hell!"

The Happy Family looked at one another dazedly. Weary drunk? *Weary*? It was unbelieveable. Such a thing had never been heard of before in the history of the Happy Family. Even Chip, who had known Weary before either had known the Flying U, could not remember anything of the sort. The Happy Family were often hilarious; they had even, on certain occasions, shot up the town; but they had done it as a family and they had done it sober. It was an unwritten law among the Flying U boys, that all riotous conduct should occur when they were together and when the Family could, as a unit, assume the consequences—if consequences there were to be.

"I guess Happy must a rode the whole blame saddle-bunch home, this time," Cal remarked, with stinging sarcasm.

"Ah, yuh can go and see fer yourselves; yuh don't need t' take *my* word fer nothing" cried Happy Jack, much grieved that they should doubt him. "I hain't had but one drink t'day—and that wasn't nothin' but beer. It's straight goods: Weary's as full as he can git and top a horse. He's sure enjoyin' himself, too. Dry Lake is all hisn—and the way he's misusin' the rights uh ownership is plumb scand'l'us. He makes me think of a cow on the fight in a forty-foot corral; nobody dast show their noses outside; Dry Lake's holed up in their sullers, till he quits camp.

"I seen him cut down on the hotel China-cook jest for tryin' t' make a sneak out t' the ice-house after some meat fer dinner. He like t' got him, too. Chink dodged behind the board-pile in the back yard, an' laid down. He was still there when I left town, and the chances is somebody else 'll have t' cook dinner t'day. Weary was so busy close-herdin' the Chinaman that I got a chanst t' sneak out the back door uh Rusty's place, climb on m' horse and take a shoot up around by the stockyards and pull fer camp. I couldn't git t' the store, so I didn't bring out no mail."

The Happy Family drew a long breath. This was getting beyond a joke.

"Looks t 'me like you fellows 'd come alive and do something about it," hinted Happy, with his mouth full. "Weary'll shoot somebody, er git shot, if he ain't took care of mighty quick."

"Happy," said Chip bluntly, "I don't grab that yarn. Weary may be in town, and he *may* be having a little fun with Dry Lake, but he isn't drunk. When you try to run a whizzer like that, you can put me down as being from Missouri."

"Same here," put in Pink, ominously soft as to voice. "Anybody that tries to make me believe Weary's performing that way has sure got his work cut out for him. If it was Happy, now—"

"Gee!" cried Jack Bates, laughing as a possible solution came to him. "I'm willing to bet money he was just stringing Happy. I'll bet he done it deliberate and with malice aforethought, just to *make* Happy sneak out uh town and burn the earth getting here so he could tell it scarey to the rest of us."

"Yeah, that's about the size of it," assented Cal.

The Family felt that they had a new one on Happy Jack, and showed it in the smiles they sent toward him.

"By golly, yes!" broke out Slim. "Weary's been layin' for Happy for a long while to pay off making the tent leak on him, that night; he's sure played a good one, this time!"

Happy carefully balanced his plate on the wagon-tongue near the doubletrees, and stood glaring down upon his tormentors.

"Aw, look here!" he began, with his voice very near to tears. Then he gulped and took a more warlike tone. "I don't set m'self up t' be a know-it-all—but I guess I can tell when a man's full uh booze. And I ain't claimin' t' be no Jiujitsu sharp" (with a meaning glance at Pink) "and I know the chances I'm takin' when I stand up agin the bunch—but I'm ready, here and now, t' fight any damn man that says I'm a liar, er that Weary was jest throwin' a load into me. Two or three uh yuh have licked me mor'n once—but that's all right. I'm willing t' back up anything I've said, and yuh can wade right in a soon as you're a mind to.

"I don't back down a darn inch. Weary's in Dry Lake. He *is* drunk. And he *is* shootin' up the town. If yuh don't want t' believe it, I guess they's no law t' make yuh—but if yuh got any sense, and are any friends uh Weary's, yuh'll mosey in and fetch him out here if yuh have t' bring him the way he brung ole Dock that time Patsy took cramps. Go on in and see fer yourselves, darn yuh! But don't go shootin' off your faces to me till yuh got a license to."

This, if unassuring, was convincing. The Happy Family stopped smiling, and looked at one another uncertainly.

"I guess two or three of you better ride in and see what there is to it," announced Chip, dryly. "If Happy is romancing—" His look was eloquent.

But Happy Jack, though he stood a good deal in awe of Chip and his sarcasm, never flinched. He looked him straight in the eye and maintained the calm of conscious innocence.

"I'll go," said Pink, getting up and throwing his plate and cup into the dishpan. "Mind yuh, I don't believe a word of it; Happy, if this is just a sell, so help me Josephine, you'll learn some brand new Jiujitsu right away quick."

"I'll go along too," Happy boldly retorted, "so if yuh want anything uh *me*, after you've saw Weary, yuh won't need t' wait till yuh strike camp t' git it. Weary loadin' me, was he? Yuh'll find out, all uh yuh, that it's *him* that's loaded."

They caught fresh horses and started—Cal, Pink, Jack Bates and Happy Jack. And Happy stood their jeers throughout the ten-mile ride with an equanimity that was new to them. For the most part he rode in silence, and grinned knowingly when they laughed too loudly at the joke Weary was playing.

"All right—maybe he is," he flung back, once. "But he sure looks the part well enough t' keep all Dry Lake indoors—and I never knowed Weary t' terrorize a hull town before. And where'd he git that horse? and where's Glory at? and why ain't he comin' on t' camp t' help you chumps giggle? Ain't he had plenty uh time t' foller me out and enjoy his little joke? And another thing, he was hard at it when I struck town. Now, where'd yuh get off at?"

To this argument they offered several explanations—at all of which

Happy grunted in great disdain.

They clattered nonchalantly into Dry Lake, still unconvinced and still jeering at Happy Jack. The town was very quiet, even for Dry Lake. As they rounded the blacksmith shop, from where they could see the whole length of the one street which the place boasted, a yell, shrill, exultant, familiar, greeted them. A long-legged figure they knew well dashed down the street to them, a waving six-shooter in one hand, the reins held aloft in the other. His horse gave evidence of hard usage, and it was a horse none of them had ever seen before.

"It's him, all right," Jack Bates admitted reluctantly.

"*Yip! Cowboys in town*!" rang the slogan of the range land. "Come on and—*wake 'em up*! *OO-oop-ee*!" He pulled up so suddenly that his horse almost sat down in the dust, and reined in beside Pink.

They eyed him in amaze, and avoided meeting one another's eyes. Truly, he was a strange-looking Weary. His head was bare and disheveled, his eyes bloodshot and glaring, his cheeks flushed hotly. His neck-kerchief covered his chest like a bib and he wore no coat; one shirtsleeve was rent from shoulder to cuff, telling eloquently that violent hands had sought to lay hold on him. His long legs, clad in Angora chaps, swung limp to the stirrup. By all these signs and tokens, they knew that he was drunk—-joyously, unequivocally, vociferously drunk!

Joe Meeker peered cautiously out of the window of Rusty Brown's place when they rode up, and Cal Emmett swore aloud at sight of him. Joe Meeker was the most indefatigable male gossip for fifty miles around, and the story of Weary's spree would spread far and fast. Worse, it would reach first of all the ears of Weary's School-ma'am, who lived at Meeker's.

Cal started to get down; he wanted to go in and reason with Joe Meeker. At all events, Ruby Satterlee must not hear of Weary's defection. It was all right, maybe, for some men to make fools of themselves in this fashion; some women would look upon it with lenience. But this was different; Weary was different, and so was Ruby Satterlee. Cal meditated upon just what would the most effectually close the mouth of Joe Meeker.

But Weary spied him as his foot touched the ground. "Oh, yuh can't sneak off like that, old-timer. Yuh stay right outside and help wake 'em up!" he shouted hoarsely.

Cal turned and looked at him keenly; looked also at the erratic movements of the gun, and reconsidered his decision. Joe Meeker could wait.

"Better come on out to camp, Weary," he said persuasively. "We're all of us going, right away. Yuh can ride out with us."

Weary had not yet extracted all the joy there was in the situation. He did not want to ride out to camp; more, he had no intention of doing so. He stood up in the stirrups and declaimed loudly his views upon the subject, and his opinion of any man who proposed such a move, and punctuated his remarks freely with profanity and bullets. Under cover of Weary's elocution Pink did a bit of jockeying and got his horse sidling up against Cal. He leaned carelessly upon the saddle-horn and fixed his big, innocent eyes upon Weary's flushed face.

"He's pretty cute, if he is full," he murmured discreetly to Cal. "He won't let his gun get empty—see? Loads after every third shot, regular. We've got to get him so excited he forgets that little ceremony. Once his gun's empty, he's all to the bad—we can take him into camp. We'll try and rush him out uh town anyway, and shoot as we go. It's our only show—unless we can get him inside and lay him out."

"Yeah, that's what we'll have to do," Cal assented guardedly. "He's sure tearing it off in large chunks, ain't he? I never knew—"

"Here! What you two gazabos making medicine about?" cried Weary suspiciously. "Break away, there. I won't stand for no side-talks—"

"We're just wondering if we hadn't all better adjourn and have something to drink," said Pink musically, straightening up in the saddle. "Come on—I'm almighty dry."

"Same here," said Jack Bates promptly taking the cue, and threw one leg over the cantle. He got no further than that.

"You stay right up on your old bench!" Weary commanded threateningly. "We're the kings uh the prairie, and we'll drink on our thrones. That so-many-kinds-of-bar-slave can pack out the dope to us. It's what he's there for."

That settled Pink's little plan to get him inside where, lined up to the bar, they might—if they were quick enough—get his gun away from him; or, failing that, the warm room and another drink or two would "lay him out" and render him harmless.

Weary, shoving three cartridges dexterously into the chambers in place of those just emptied, shouted to Rusty to bring out the "sheepdip." The four drew together and attempted further consultation, separated hastily when his eye fell upon them, and waited meekly his further pleasure. They knew better than to rouse his anger against them.

Weary, displeased because Rusty did not immediately respond to his call, sent a shot or two through the window by way of hurrying him.

Whereupon Rusty cautiously opened the door, shoved a tray with bottle and glasses ostentatiously out into the sunlight for a peace offering, and finding that hostilities ceased, came forth in much fear and served them.

They drank solemnly.

"Take another one, darn yuh," commanded Weary.

They drank again, more solemnly.

The sun beat harshly down upon the deserted street, and upon the bare, tousled, brown head of Weary. The four stared at him uneasily; they had never seen him like this before, and it gave him an odd, unfamiliar air that worried them more than they would have cared to own.

Only Pink refused to lose heart. "Well, come on—let's wake up these dead ones," he shouted, drawing his gun and firing into the air. "Get busy, you sleepers! *Yip*! *Cowboys in town*!" He wheeled and darted off down the street, shooting and yelling, and the others, with Weary in their midst, followed. At the blacksmith shop, Pink, tacitly the leader of the rescuers, would have gone straight on out of town. But Weary whirled and galloped back, firing merrily into the air. A bit chagrined, Pink wheeled and galloped at his heels, fuming inwardly at the methodical reloading after every third shot. Cal, on the other side, glanced across at Pink, shook his head ruefully and shoved more shells into his smoking gun.

Back and forth from the store at one end of the street to the blacksmith shop at the other they rode, yelling till their throats ached and shooting till their gun-barrels were hot; and Weary kept pace with them and out-yelled and out-shot the most energetic, and never once forgot the little ceremony of shoving in fresh shells after the third shot. Drunk, Weary appeared much more cautious than when sober. Pink grew hot and hoarse, and counted the shots, one, two, three, over and over till his brain grew sick.

On the seventh trip down the street, a sleek, black head appeared for an instant over the top of the board-pile in the hotel yard. A pair of frightened, slant eyes peered out at them. Weary, just about to reload, caught sight of him and gave a whoop of pure joy.

"Lord, how I do hate a Chink!" he cried, and dropped to the ground the three shells in his hand that he might fire the two in his gun.

Pink yelled also. "Nab him, Cal!" and caught his gun arm the instant

Weary's last bullet left the barrel.

Cal leaned and caught Weary round the neck in a close hug. Jack Bates and Happy Jack crowded close, eager to help but finding no place to take hold.

"Now, you blame fool, come along home and quit disgracing the whole community!" cried Cal, half angrily. "Ain't yuh got any sense at all?"

Weary protested; he swore; he threatened. He was not in the least like his old, sweet-tempered self. He mourned openly because he had no longer a gun that he might slay and spare not. He insisted that he would take much pleasure in killing them all off—especially Pink. He felt that Pink was the greatest traitor in the lot, and said that it would be a special joy to him to see Pink expire slowly and in great pain. He remarked that they would be sorry, before they were through with him, and repeated, many times, the hint that he never forgot a friend or forgave an enemy—and looked darkly at Pink.

"You're batty," Pink told him sorrowfully, the while they led him out through the lane. "We're the best friends yuh got—only yuh don't appreciate us."

Weary glared at him through a tangle of brown hair, and remarked further, in tones that one could hear a mile, upon the subject of Pink's treachery and the particular kind of death he deserved to die.

Pink shrugged his shoulder and grew sulky; then, old friendship growing strong within him, he sought to soothe him.

But Weary absolutely declined to be soothed. Cal, serene in his fancied favoritism, attempted the impossible, and was greeted with language which no man living had ever before heard from the lips of Weary the sunny. Jack Bates and Happy Jack, profiting by his experience, wisely kept silence.

For this, the homeward ride was not the companionable gallop it usually was. They tried to learn from Weary what he had done with Glory, and whence came the mud-colored cayuse with the dim, blotched brand, that he bestrode. They asked also where were the horses he had been sent to bring.

In return, Weary began viciously to dissect their pedigree and general moral characters.

After that, they gave over trying to question or to reason, and the last two miles they rode in utter silence. Weary, tiring of venom that brought no results, subsided gradually into mutterings, and then into sullen silence, so that, save for his personal appearance, they reached camp quite decorously.

Chip met them at the bed wagon, where they slipped dispiritedly off their horses and began to unsaddle—all save Weary; he stared around him, got cautiously to the ground and walked, with that painfully circumspect stride sometimes affected by the intoxicated, over to the cook-tent.

"Well," snapped Chip to the others, "For once in his life, Happy was right."

Weary, still planting his feet primly upon the trampled grass, went smiling up to the stupefied Patsy.

"Lord, how I do love a big, fat, shiny Dutch cook!" he murmured, and flung his long arms around him in a hug that caused Patsy to grunt. "How yuh was, already, Dutchy? Got any pie in this man's cow-camp?"

Patsy scowled and drew haughtily away from his embrace; there was one thing he would not endure, even from Weary: it was having his nationality too lightly mentioned. To call him Dutchy was a direct insult, and the Happy Family never did it to his face—unless the provocation was very great. To call him Dutchy and in the same breath to ask for pie—that, indeed, went far beyond the limits of decency.

"Py cosh, you not ged any pie, Weary Davidson. Py cosh, I learns you not to call names py sober peoples. You not get no grub whiles you iss too drunk to be decend mit folks."

"Hey? Yuh won't feed a man when he's hungry? Yuh darn Dutch—" Weary went into details in a way that was surprising.

The Happy Family rushed up and pulled him off Patsy before he had done any real harm, and held him till the cook had got into the shelter of his tent and armed himself with a frying pan. Weary was certainly outdoing himself today. The Happy Family resolved into a peace committee.

"Aw, dig up some pie for him, Patsy," pleaded Cal. "Yuh don't want to mind anything he says while he's like this; yuh know Weary's a good friend to yuh when he's sober. Get some strong coffee—that'll straighten him out."

"Py cosh, I not feed no drunk fools. I not care if it iss Weary. He hit mine jaw—"

"Aw, gwan! I guess yuh never get that way yourself," put in Happy Jack, ponderously sarcastic. "I guess yuh never tanked up in roundup, one time, and left me cook chuck fer the hull outfit—and I guess Weary never rode all night, and had the dickens of a time, tryin' t' get yuh a doctor—yuh old heathen. Yuh sure are an ungrateful cuss."

"Give him some good, hot coffee, Patsy, and anything he wants to eat," commanded Chip, more sharply than was his habit. "And don't be all day about it, either."

That settled it, of course; Chip, being foreman, was to be obeyed—unless Patsy would rather roll his blankets and hunt a new job. He took to muttering weird German sentences the while he brought out two pies and poured black coffee into a cup. The reveler drank the coffee— three cups of it—ate a whole blueberry pie, and was consoled. He even wanted to embrace Patsy again, but was restrained by the others. After that he went over and laid down in the shade of the bed-wagon, and straightway began to snore with much energy and enthusiasm.

Chip watched him a minute and then went and sat down on the shady side of the bed-tent and began gloomily to roll a cigarette. The rest of the Happy Family silently followed his example; for a long while no one said a word. It certainly was a shock to see Weary like that. Not because it is unusual for a man of the range to get in that condition—for on the contrary, it is rather commonplace. And the Happy Family had lived the life too long to judge a man harshly because of an occasional indiscreet departure from the path virtuous; they knew that the man might be a good fellow, after all. In the West grows Charity sturdily, with branches quite broad enough to cover certain defections on the part of such men as Weary Davidson.

For that, the real shock came in the utter unexpectedness of the thing—and from the fact that a man, even though prone to indulge in such riotous conduct, is supposed to forswear such indulgence when he has other and more important things to do. Weary had been sent afar on a matter of business; he had ridden Glory, a horse belonging to the Flying U. His arrival without the strays he had been sent after; without even the horse he had ridden away—that was the real disaster. He had broken a trust; he had, apparently, appropriated a horse that did not belong to him, which was worse. But the Happy Family were loyal, to a man. They did not condemn him; they were only waiting for him to sleep himself into a condition to explain the mystery.

"Somebody's doped him," said Pink with decision, after three hours of shying around the subject. "You'll see; somebody's doped him and likely took Glory away when they'd got him batty enough not to know the difference. Yuh mind the queer look in his eyes? And he acts queer. So help me Josephine! I'd sure like to get next to the man that traded horses with him."

The Happy Family breathed deeply; they were all, apparently, thinking the same thing.

"By golly, that's what," spoke Slim, with decision. "He does act like a man that had been doped."

"Whisky straight wouldn't make that much difference in a man," averred Jack Bates. "Yuh can't *get* Weary on the fight, hardly, when he's sober; and look at the way he was in town—hot to slaughter that Chinaman that wasn't doing a thing to him, and saying how he hated Chinks. Weary don't; he always says, when Patsy don't make enough pie to go round, that if he was running the outfit he'd have a Chink to cook."

"Aw, look at the way he acted t' Rusty—and he thinks a lot uh Rusty, too," put in Happy Jack, who felt the importance of discovery and was in an unusually complacent mood. "And he was going t' hang Pink up by the heels and—"

Pink turned round and looked at him fixedly, and Happy Jack became suddenly interested in his cigarette.

"Say, he'll sure be sore when he comes to himself, though," observed Cal. "I don't know how he's going to square himself with his school-ma'am. Joe Meeker was into Rusty's place while the big setting comes off; I would uh given him a gentle hint about keeping his face closed, only Weary wouldn't let me off my horse. Joe'll sure give a high-colored picture uh the performance."

"Well, if he does, he'll regret it a lot," prophesied Pink. "And anyway, something sure got wrong with Weary; do yuh suppose he'd give up Glory deliberately? Not on your life! Glory comes next to the Schoolma'am in his affections."

"Wonder where he got that dirt-colored cayuse, anyhow," mused Cal.

"I was studying out the brand, a while ago," Pink answered. "It's blotched pretty bad, but I made it out. It's the Rocking R—they range down along Milk River, next to the reservation. I've never had anything to do with the outfit, but I'd gamble on the brand, all right."

"Well, how the deuce would he come by a Rocking R horse? He never got it around here, anywheres. He must uh got it up on the Marias."

"Then that must be a good long jag he's had—which I don't believe," interjected Cal.

"Somebody," said Pink meaningly, "ought to have gone along with him; this thing wouldn't uh happened, then."

"Ye-e-s?" Chip felt that the remark applied to him as a foreman, rather than as one of the Family, and he resented it. "If I'd sent somebody else with him, the outfit would probably be out two horses, instead of one—and there'd be two men under the bed-wagon with their hats and coats missing."

Pink's eyes, under their heavy fringe of curled lashes, turned ominously purple. "With all due respect to you, Mr. Bennett, I'd like to have you explain—"

A horseman rode quietly up to them from behind a thicket of choke-cherry bushes. Pink, catching sight of him first, stopped short off and stared.

"Hello, boys," greeted the new-comer gaily. "How's everything? Mamma! it's good to get amongst white folks again."

The Happy Family rose up as one man and stared fixedly; not one of them spoke, or moved. Pink was the first to recover.

"Well—I'll be—damned!"

"Yuh sure will, Cadwolloper, if yuh don't let down them pretty lashes and quit gawping. What the dickens ails you fellows, anyhow? Is—is my hat on crooked, or—or anything?"

"Weary, by all that's good!" murmured Chip, dazedly.

Weary swung a long leg over the back of Glory and came to earth. "Say," he began in the sunny, drawly voice that was good to hear, "what's the joke?"

The Happy Family sat down again and looked queerly at one another.

Happy Jack glanced furtively at a long figure in the grass near by, and then, unhappily, at Weary.

"It's him, all right," he blurted solemnly. "They're both him!"

The Happy Family snickered hysterically.

Weary took a long step and confronted Happy Jack. "I'm both him, am I?" he repeated mockingly. "Mamma, but you're a lucid cuss!" He turned and regarded the stunned Family judicially.

"If there's any of it left," he hinted sweetly, "I wouldn't mind taking a jolt myself; but from the looks, and the actions, yuh must have got away with at least two gallons!"

"Oh, we can give you a jolt, I guess," Chip retorted dryly. "Just step this way."

Weary, wondering a bit at the tone of him, followed; at his heels came the perturbed Happy Family. Chip stooped and turned the sleeping one over on his back; the sleeper opened his eyes and blinked questioningly up at the huddle of bent faces.

The astonished, blue eyes of Weary met the quizzical blue eyes of his other self. He leaned against the wagon wheel. "Oh, mamma!" he said, weakly.

His other self sat up and looked around, felt for his hat, saw that it was gone, and reached mechanically for his cigarette material.

"By the Lord! Are punchers so damn scarce in this neck uh the woods, that yuh've got to shanghai a man in order to make a full crew?" he demanded of the Happy Family, in the voice of Weary—minus the drawl. "I've got a string uh cayuses in that darn stockyards, back in town—and a damn poor town it is!—and I've also got a date with the Circle roundup for tomorrow night. What yuh going to do about it? Speak up, for I'm in a hurry to know."

The Happy Family looked at one another and said nothing.

"Say," began Weary, mildly. "Did yuh say your name was Ira Mallory, and do yuh mind how they used to mix us up in school, when we were both kids? 'Cause I've got a hunch you're the same irrepressible that has the honor to be my cousin."

"I didn't say it," retorted his other self, pugnaciously. "But I don't know as it's worth while denying it. If you're Will Davidson, shake. What the devil d'yuh want to look so much like me, for? Ain't yuh got any manners? Yuh always was imitating your betters." He grinned and got slowly to his feet. "Boys, I don't know yuh, but I've a hazy recollection that we had one hell of a time shooting up that little townerine, back there. I don't go on a limb very often, but when I do, folks are apt to find it out right away."

The Happy Family laughed.

"By golly," said Slim slowly, "that cousin story 's all right—but I bet yuh you two fellows are twins, at the very least!"

"Guess again, Slim," cried Weary, already in the clutch of old times. "Run away and play, you kids. Irish and me have got steen things to talk about, and mustn't be bothered."

THE UNHEAVENLY TWINS

There was a dead man's estate to be settled, over beyond the Bear Paws, and several hundred head of cattle and horses had been sold to the highest bidder, who was Chip Bennett, of the Flying U. Later, there were the cattle and horses to be gathered and brought to the home range; and Weary, always Chip's choice when came need of a trusted man, was sent to bring them. He was to hire what men he needed down there, work the range with the Rocking R, and bring home the stock—when his men could take the train and go back whence they had come. The Happy Family was disappointed. Pink and Irish, especially, had hoped to be sent along; for both knew well the range north of the Bear Paws, and both would like to have made the trip with Weary. But men were scarce and the Happy Family worked well together—so well that Chip grudged every man of them that ever had to be sent afar. So Weary went alone, and Pink and Irish watched him wistfully when he rode away and were extremely unpleasant companions for the rest of that day, at least. Over beyond the Bear Paws men seemed scarcer even than around the Flying U range. Weary scouted fruitlessly for help, wasted two days in the search, and then rode to Bullhook and sent this wire—collect—to Chip, and grinned as he wondered how much it would cost. He, too, had rather resented being sent off down there alone.

"C. BENNETT, Dry Lake: Can't get a man here for love or money. Have tried both, and held one up with a gun. No use. Couldn't top a saw horse. For the Lord's sake, send somebody I know. I want Irish and Pink and Happy—and I want them bad. Get a move on. W. DAVIDSON."

Chip grinned when he read it, paid the bill, and told the three to get ready to hit the trail. And the three grinned answer and immediately became very busy; hitting the trail, in this case, meant catching the next train out of Dry Lake, for there were horses bought with the cattle, and much time would be saved by making up an outfit down there.

Weary rode dispiritedly into Sleepy Trail (which Irish usually spoke of as Camas, because it had but lately been rechristened to avoid conflictions with another Camas farther up on Milk River). Weary thought, as he dismounted from Glory, which he had brought with him from home, that Sleepy Trail fitted the place exactly, and that whenever he heard Irish refer to it as Camas, he would call him down and make him use this other and more appropriate title.

Sleepy it was, in that hazy sunshine of mid fore-noon, and apparently deserted. He tied Glory to the long hitching pole where a mild-eyed gray stood dozing on three legs, and went striding, rowels a-clank, into the saloon. He had not had any answer to his telegram, and the world did not look so very good to him. He did not know that Pink and Irish and Happy Jack were even then speeding over the prairies on the eastbound train from Dry Lake, to meet him. He had come to Sleepy Trail to wait for the next stage, on a mere hope of some message from the Flying U.

The bartender looked up, gave a little, welcoming whoop and leaned half over the bar, hand extended. "Hello, Irish! Lord! When did *you* get back?"

Weary smiled and shook the hand with much emphasis. Irish had once created a sensation in Dry Lake by being taken for Weary; Weary wondered if, in the guise of Irish, there might not be some diversion for him here in Sleepy Trail. He remembered the maxim "Turn about is fair play," and immediately acted thereon.

"I just came down from the Flying U the other day," he said.

The bartender half turned, reached a tall, ribbed bottle and two glasses, and set them on the bar before Weary. "Go to it," he invited cordially. "I'll gamble yuh brought your thirst right along with yuh—and that's your pet brand. Back to stay?"

Weary poured himself a modest "two fingers," and wondered if he had better claim to have reformed; Irish could—and did—drink long and deep, where Weary indulged but moderately.

"No," he said, setting the glass down without refilling. "They sent me back on business. How's everything?"

The bartender spoke his wonder at the empty glass, listened while Weary explained how he had cut down his liquid refreshments "just to see how it would go, and which was boss," and then told much unmeaning gossip about men and women Weary had never heard of before.

Weary listened with exaggerated interest, and wondered what the fellow would do if he told him he was not Irish Mallory at all. He reflected, with some amusement, that he did not even know what to call the bartender, and tried to remember if Irish had ever mentioned him. He was about to state quietly that he had never met him before, and watch the surprise of the other, when the bartender grew more interesting.

"And say! yuh'd best keep your gun strapped on yuh, whilst you're down here," he told Weary, with some earnestness. "Spikes Weber is in this country—come just after yuh left; fact is, he's got it into his block that you left *because* he come. Brought his wife along—say! I feel sorry for that little woman—and when he ain't bowling up and singing his war-song about you, and all he'll do when he meets up with yuh, he's dealing her misery and keeping cases that nobody runs off with her. Why, at dances, he won't let her dance with nobody but him! Goes plumb wild, sometimes, when it's 'change partners' in a square dance, and he sees her swingin' with somebody he thinks looks good to her. I've saw him raising hell with her, off in some corner between dances, and her trying not to let on she's cryin'. He's dead sure you're still crazy over her, and ready to steal her away from him first chance, only you're afraid uh him. He never gits full but he reads out your pedigree to the crowd. So I just thought I'd tell you, and let yuh be on your guard."

"Thanks," said Weary, getting out papers and tobacco. "And whereabouts will I find this lovely specimen uh manhood?"

"They're stopping over to Bill Mason's; but yuh better not go hunting trouble, Irish. That's the worst about putting yuh next to the lay. You sure do love a fight. But I thought I'd let yuh know, as a friend, so he wouldn't take you unawares. Don't be a fool and go out looking for him, though; he ain't worth the trouble."

"I won't," Weary promised generously. "I haven't lost nobody that looks like Spikes-er-" he searched his memory frantically for the other name, failed to get it, and busied himself with his cigarette, looking mean and bloodthirsty to make up. "Still," he added darkly, "if I should happen to meet up with him, yuh couldn't blame me—"

"Oh, sure not!" the bartender hastened to cut in. "It'd be a case uh self-defence—the way he's been makin' threats. But—"

"Maybe," hazarded Weary mildly, "you'd kinda like to see—*her*—a widow?"

"From all accounts," the other retorted, flushing a bit nevertheless, "If yuh make her a widow, yuh won't leave her that way long. I've heard it said you was pretty far gone, there."

Weary considered, the while he struck another match and relighted his cigarette. He had not expected to lay bare any romance in the somewhat tumultuous past of Irish. Irish had not seemed the sort of fellow who had an unhappy love affair to dream of nights; he had seemed a particularly whole-hearted young man.

"Well, yuh see," he said vaguely, "Maybe I've got over it." The bartender regarded him fixedly and unbelievingly. "You'll have quite a contract making Spikes swallow that," he remarked drily.

"Oh, damn Spikes," murmured Weary, with the fine recklessness of Irish in his tone.

At that moment a cowboy jangled in, caught sight of Weary's back and fell upon him joyously, hailing him as Irish. Weary was very glad to see him, and listened assiduously for something that would give him a clue to the fellow's identity. In the meantime he called him "Say, Old-timer," and "Cully." It had come to be a self-instituted point of honor to play the game through without blundering. He waved his hand hospitably toward the ribbed bottle, and told the stranger to "Throw into yuh, Old-timer—it's on me." And when Old-timer straightway began doing so, Weary leaned against the bar and wiped his forehead, and wondered who the dickens the fellow could be. In Dry Lake, Irish had been—well, hilarious—and not accountable for any little peculiarities. In Sleepy Trail Weary was, perhaps he considered unfortunately, sober and therefore obliged to feel his way carefully.

"Say! yuh want to keep your eyes peeled for Spikes Weber, Irish," remarked the unknown, after two drinks. "He's pawing up the earth whenever he hears your name called. He's sure anxious to see the sod packed down nice on top uh yuh."

"So I heard; his nibs here," indicating the bartender, "has been wising me up, a lot. When's the stage due, tomorrow, Oldtimer?" Weary was getting a bit ashamed of addressing them both impartially in that manner, but it was the best he could do, not knowing the names men called them. In this instance he spoke to the bartender.

"Why, yuh going to pull out while your hide's whole?" bantered the cowboy, with the freedom which long acquaintance breeds.

"I've got business out uh town, and I want to be back time the stage pulls in."

"Well, Limpy's still holding the ribbons over them buckskins uh his, and he ain't varied five minutes in five years," responded the bartender. "So I guess yuh can look for him same old time."

Weary's eyes opened a bit wider, then drooped humorously. "Oh, all right," he murmured, as though thoroughly enlightened rather than being rather more in the dark than before. In the name of Irish he found it expedient to take another modest drink, and then excused himself with a "See yuh later, boys," and went out and mounted Glory.

Ten miles nearer the railroad—which at that was not what even a Montanan would call close—he had that day established headquarters and was holding a bunch of saddle horses pending the arrival of help. He rode out on the trail thoughtfully, a bit surprised that he had not found the situation more amusing. To be taken for Irish was a joke, and to learn thereby of Irish's little romance should be funny. But it wasn't.

Weary wondered how Irish got mixed up in a deal like that, which somehow did not seem to be in line with his character. And he wished, a bit vindictively, that this Spikes Weber *could* meet Irish. He rather thought that Spikes needed the chastening effects of such a meeting. Weary, while not in the least quarrelsome on his own account, was ever the staunch defender of a friend.

Just where another brown trail branched off and wandered away over a hill to the east, a woman rode out and met him face to face. She pulled up and gave a little cry that brought Weary involuntarily to a halt.

"You!" she exclaimed, in a tone that Weary felt he had no right to hear from any but his little schoolma'am. "But I knew you'd come back when you heard I—Have—have you seen Spikes, Ira?"

Weary flushed embarrassment; this was no joke. "No," he stammered, in some doubt just how to proceed. "The fact is, you've made a little mistake. I'm not—"

"Oh, you needn't go on," she interrupted, and her voice, had Weary known it better, heralded the pouring out of a woman's heart. "I know I've made a mistake, all right; you don't need to tell me that. And I suppose you want to tell me that you've got over—things; that you don't care, any more. Maybe you don't, but it'll take a lot to make me believe it. Because you *did* care, Ira. You *cared*, all right enough!" She laughed in the way that makes one very uncomfortable.

"And maybe you'll tell me that I didn't. But I did, and I do yet. I ain't ashamed to say it, if I did marry Spikes Weber just to spite you. That's all it was, and you'd have found it out if you hadn't gone off the way you did. I *hate* Spikes Weber; and he knows it, Ira. He knows I—care—for you, and he's making my life a hell. Oh, maybe I deserve it— but you won't— Now you've come back, you can have it out with him; and I—I almost hope you'll kill him! I do, and I don't care if it is wicked. I—I don't care for anything much, but—you." She had big, soft brown eyes, and a sweet, weak mouth, and she stopped and looked at Weary in a way that he could easily imagine would be irresistible—to a man who cared.

Weary felt that he was quite helpless. She had hurried out sentences that sealed his lips. He could not tell her now that she had made a mistake; that he was not Ira Mallory, but a perfect stranger. The only thing to do now was to carry the thing through as tactfully as possible, and get away as soon as he could. Playing he was Irish, he found, was not without its disadvantages.

"What particular brand of hell has he been making for you?" he asked her sympathetically.

"I wouldn't think, knowing Spikes as you do, you'd need to ask," she said impatiently. "The same old brand, I guess. He gets drunk, and then—I told him, right out, just after we were married, that I liked you the best, and he don't forget it; and he don't let me. He swears he'll shoot you on sight—as if that would do any good! He hates you, Ira." She laughed again unpleasantly.

Weary, sitting uneasily in the saddle looking at her, wondered if Irish really cared; or if, in Weary's place, he would have sat there so calmly and just looked at her. She was rather pretty, in a pink and white, weak way. He could easily imagine her marrying Spikes Weber for mere spite; what he could not imagine, was Irish in love with her.

It seemed almost as if she caught a glimmer of his thoughts, for she reined closer, and her teeth were digging into her lower lip. "Well, aren't you going to *do* anything?" she demanded desperately. "You're here, and I've told you I—care. Are you going to leave me to bear Spikes' abuse always?"

"You married him," Weary remarked mildly and a bit defensively. It seemed to him that loyalty to Irish impelled him.

She tossed her head contemptuously. "It's nice to throw that at me. I might get back at you and say you loved me. You did, you know."

"And you married Spikes; what can *I* do about it?"

"What—can—you—do—about it? Did you come back to ask me that?" There was a well defined, white line around her mouth, and her eyes were growing ominously bright. Weary did not like the look of her, nor her tone. He felt, somehow, glad that it was not Irish, but himself; Irish might have felt the thrall of old times—whatever they were—and have been tempted. His eyes, also, grew ominous, but his voice was very smooth. (Irish, too, had that trait of being quietest when he was most roused.)

"I came back on business; I will confess I didn't come to see you," he said. "I'm only a bone-headed cowpuncher, but even cowpunchers can play square. They don't, as a rule step in between a man and his wife. You married Spikes, and according to your own tell, you did it to spite me. So I say again, what can *I* do about it?"

She looked at him dazedly.

"Uh course," he went on gently, "I won't stand to see any man abuse his wife, or bandy her name or mine around the country. If I should happen to meet up with Spikes, there'll likely be some dust raised. And if I was you, and Spikes abused me, I'd quit him cold."

"Oh, I see," she said sharply, with an exaggeration of scorn. "You have got over it, then. There's someone else. I might have known a man can't be trusted to care for the same woman long. You ran after me and acted the fool, and kept on till you made me believe you really meant all you said—"

"And you married Spikes," Weary reiterated— ungenerously, perhaps; but it was the only card he felt sure of. There was no gainsaying that fact, it seemed. She had married Spikes in a fit of pique at Irish. Still, it was not well to remind her of it too often. In the next five minutes of tumultuous recrimination, Weary had cause to remember what Shakespeare has to say about a woman scorned, and he wondered, more than ever, if Irish had really cared. The girl—even now he did not know what name to call her—was showing a strain of coarse temper; the temper that must descend to personalities and the calling of unflattering names. Weary, not being that type of male human who can retort in kind, sat helpless and speechless the while she berated him. When at last he found opportunity for closing the interview and riding on, her anger-sharpened voice followed him shrewishly afar. Weary breathed deep relief when the distance swallowed it, and lifted his gray hat to wipe his beaded forehead. "Mamma mine!" he said fervently to Glory. "Irish was sure playing big luck when she *did* marry Spikes; and I don't wonder at the poor devil taking to drink. I would, too, if my little schoolma'am—"

At the ranch, he hastened to make it quite plain that he was not Ira Mallory, but merely his cousin, Will Davidson. He was quite determined to put a stop to all this annoying mixing up of identities. And as for Spikes Weber, since meeting the woman Spikes claimed from him something very like sympathy; only Weary had no mind to stand calmly and hear Irish maligned by anybody.

The next day he rode again to Sleepy Trail to meet the stage, hoping fervently that he would get some word—and that favorable—from Chip. He was thinking, just then, a great deal about his own affairs and not at all about the affairs of Irish. So that he was inside the saloon before he remembered that the bartender knew him for Irish.

The bartender nodded to him in friendly fashion, and jerked his head warningly toward a far corner where two men sat playing seven-up half-heartedly. Weary looked, saw that both were strangers, and puzzled a minute over the mysterious gesture of the bartender. It did not occur to him, just then, that one of the men might be Spikes Weber.

The man who was facing him nipped the corners of the cards idly together and glanced up; saw Weary standing there with an elbow on the bar looking at him, and pushed back his chair with an oath unmistakably warlike. Weary resettled his hat and looked mildly surprised. The bartender moved out of range and watched breathlessly.

"You —— —— ————!" swore Spikes Weber, coming truculently forward, hand to hip. He was of medium height and stockily built, with the bull neck and little, deep-set eyes that go often with a nature quarrelsome.

Weary still leaned his elbow on the bar and smiled at him tolerantly.

"Feel bad anywhere?" he wanted to know, when the other was very close.

Spikes Weber, from very surprise, stopped and regarded Weary for a space before he began swearing again. His hand was still at his hip, but the gun it touched remained in his pocket. Plainly, he had not expected just this attitude.

Weary waited, smothering a yawn, until the other finished a particularly pungent paragraph. "A good jolt uh brandy 'll sometimes cure a bad case uh colic," he remarked. "Better have our friend here fix yuh up—but it'll be on you. I ain't paying for drinks just now."

Spikes snorted and began upon the pedigree and general character of Irish. Weary took his elbow off the bar, and his eyes lost their sunniness and became a hard blue, darker than was usual. It took a good deal to rouse Weary to the fighting point, and it is saying much for the tongue of Spikes that Weary was roused thoroughly.

"That'll be about enough," he said sharply, cutting short a sentence from the other. "I kinda hated to start in and take yuh all to pieces—but yuh better saw off right there, or I can't be responsible—"

A gun barrel caught the light menacingly, and Weary sprang like the pounce of a cat, wrested the gun from the hand of Spikes and rapped him smartly over the head with the barrel. "Yuh would, eh?" he snarled, and tossed the gun upon the bar, where the bartender caught it as it slid along the smooth surface and put it out of reach.

After that, chairs went spinning out of the way, and glasses jingled to the impact of a body striking the floor with much force. Came the slapping sound of hammering fists and the scuffling of booted feet, together with the hard breathing of fighting men.

Spikes, on his back, looked up into the blazing eyes he thought were the eyes of Irish and silently acknowledged defeat. But Weary would not let it go at that.

"Are yuh whipped to a finish, so that yuh don't want any more trouble with anybody?" he wanted to know.

Spikes hesitated but the fraction of a second before he growled a reluctant yes.

"Are yuh a low-down, lying sneak of a woman-fighter, that ain't got nerve enough to stand up square to a ten-year-old boy?"

Spikes acknowledged that he was. Before the impromptu catechism was ended, Spikes had acknowledged other and more humiliating things—to the delectation of the bartender, the stage driver and two or three men of leisure who were listening.

When Spikes had owned to being every mean, unknowable thing that Weary could call to mind—and his imagination was never of the barren sort—Weary generously permitted him to get upon his feet and skulk out to where his horse was tied. After that, Weary gave his unruffled attention to the stage driver and discovered the unwelcome fact that there was no letter and no telegram for one William Davidson, who looked a bit glum when he heard it.

So he, too, went out and mounted Glory and rode away to the ranch where waited the horses; and as he went he thought, for perhaps the first time in his life, some hard and unflattering things of Chip Bennett. He had never dreamed Chip would calmly overlook his needs and leave him in the lurch like this.

At the ranch, when he had unsaddled Glory and gone to the bunk-house, he discovered Irish, Pink and Happy Jack wrangling amicably over whom a certain cross-eyed girl on the train had been looking at most of the time. Since each one claimed all the glances for himself, and since there seemed no possible way of settling the dispute, they gave over the attempt gladly when Weary appeared, and wanted to know, first thing, who or what had been gouging the hide off his face.

Weary, not aware until the moment that he was wounded, answered that he had done it shaving; at which the three hooted derision and wanted to know since when he had taken to shaving his nose. Weary smiled inscrutably and began talking of something else until he had weaned them from the subject, and learned that they had bribed the stage driver to let them off at this particular ranch; for the stage driver knew Irish, and knew also that a man he had taken to be Irish was making this place his headquarters. The stage driver was one of those male gossips who know everything.

When he could conveniently do so, Weary took Irish out of hearing of the others and told him about Spikes Weber. Irish merely swore. After that, Weary told him about Spikes Weber's wife, in secret fear and with much tact, but in grim detail. Irish listened with never a word to say.

"I done what looked to me the best thing, under the circumstances," Weary apologized at the last, "and I hope I haven't mixed yuh up a bunch uh trouble. Mamma mine! she's sure on the fight, though, and she's got a large, black opinion of yuh as a constant lover. If yuh want to square yourself with her, Irish, you've got a big contract."

"I don't want to square myself," Irish retorted, grinning a bit. "I did have it bad, I admit; but when she went and got tied up to Spikes, that cured me right off. She's kinda pretty, and girls were scarce, and—oh, hell! you know how it goes with a man. I'd a married her and found out afterwards that her mind was like a little paper windmill stuck up on the gatepost with a shingle nail—only she saved me the trouble. Uh course, I was some sore over the deal for awhile; but I made up my mind long ago that Spikes was the only one in the bunch that had any sympathy coming. If he's been acting up like you say, I change the verdict: there ain't anything coming to him but a big bunch uh trouble. I'm much obliged to yuh, Weary; you done me a good turn and earnt a lot uh gratitude, which is yours for keeps. Wonder if supper ain't about due; I've the appetite of a Billy goat, if anybody should ask yuh."

At supper Irish was uncommonly silent, and did some things without thinking; such as pouring a generous stream of condensed cream into his coffee. Weary, knowing well that Irish drank his coffee without cream, watched him a bit closer than he would otherwise have done; Irish was the sort of man who does not always act by rule.

After supper Weary missed him quite suddenly, and went to the door of the bunk-house to see where he had gone. He did not see Irish, but on a hilltop, in the trail that led to Sleepy Trail, he saw a flurry of dust. Two minutes of watching saw it drift out of sight over the hill, which proved that the maker was traveling rapidly away from the ranch. Weary settled his hat down to his eyebrows and went out to find the foreman.

The foreman, down at the stable, said that Irish had borrowed a horse from him, unsacked his saddle as if he were in a hurry about something, and had pulled out on a high lope. No, he had not told the foreman where he was headed for, and the foreman knew Irish too well to ask. Yes, now Weary spoke of it, Irish did have his gun buckled on him, and he headed for Sleepy Trail.

Weary waited for no further information. He threw his saddle on a horse that he knew could get out and drift, if need came: presently he, too, was chasing a brown dust cloud over the hill toward Sleepy Trail.

That Irish had gone to find Spikes Weber, Weary was positive; that Spikes was not a man who could be trusted to fight fair, he was even more positive. Weary, however, was not afraid for Irish—he was merely a bit uneasy and a bit anxious to be on hand when came the meeting. He spurred along the trail darkening with the afterglow of a sun departed and night creeping down upon the land, and wondered whether he would be able to come up with Irish before he reached town.

At the place where the trail forked—the place where he had met the wife of Spikes, he saw from a distance another rider gallop out of the dusk and follow in the way that Irish had gone. Without other evidence than mere instinct, he knew the horseman for Spikes. When, further along, the horseman left the trail and angled away down a narrow coulee, Weary rode a bit faster. He did not know the country very well, and was not sure of where that coulee led; but he knew the nature of a man like Spikes Weber, and his uneasiness was not lulled at the sight. He meant to overtake Irish, if he could; after that he had no plan whatever.

When, however, he came to the place where Spikes had turned off. Weary turned off also and followed down the coulee; and he did not explain why, even to himself. He only hurried to overtake the other, or at least to keep him in sight.

The darkness lightened to bright starlight, with a moon not yet in its prime to throw shadows black and mysterious against the coulee sides. The coulee itself, Weary observed, was erratic in the matter of height, width and general direction. Places there were where the width dwindled until there was scant room for the cow trail his horse conscientiously followed; places there were where the walls were easy slopes to climb, and others where the rocks hung, a sheer hundred feet, above him.

One of the easy slopes came near throwing him off the trail of Spikes. He climbed the slope, and Weary would have ridden by, only that he caught a brief glimpse of something on the hilltop; something that moved, and that looked like a horseman. Puzzled but persistent, Weary turned back where the slope was easiest, and climbed also. He did not know the country well enough to tell, in that come-and-go light made uncertain by drifting clouds, just where he was or where he would bring up; he only knew instinctively that where Spikes rode, trouble rode also.

Quite suddenly at the last came further knowledge. It was when, still following, he rode along a steeply sloping ridge that narrowed perceptibly, that he looked down, down, and saw, winding brownly in the starlight, a trail that must be the trail he had left at the coulee head.

"Mamma!" he ejaculated softly, and strained eyes under his hatbrim to glimpse the figure he knew rode before. Then, looking down again, he saw a horseman galloping rapidly towards the ridge, and pulled up short when he should have done the opposite—for it was then that seconds counted.

When the second glance showed the horseman to be Irish, Weary drove in his spurs and galloped forward. Ten leaps perhaps he made, when a rifle shot came sharply ahead. He glanced down and saw horse and rider lying, a blotch of indefinable shape, in the trail. Weary drew his own gun and went on, his teeth set tight together. Now, when it was too late, he understood thoroughly the situation.

He came clattering out of the gloom to the very, point of the bluff, just where it was highest and where it crowded closest the trail a long hundred feet below. A man stood there on the very edge, with a rifle in his hands. He may have been crouching, just before, but now he was standing erect, looking fixedly down at the dark heap in the trail below, and his figure, alert yet unwatchful, was silhouetted sharply against the sky.

When Weary, gun at aim, charged furiously down upon him, he whirled, ready to give battle for his life; saw the man he supposed was lying down there dead in the trail, and started backward with a yell of pure terror. "Irish!" He toppled, threw the rifle from him in a single convulsive movement and went backward, down and down.—

Weary got off his horse and, gun still gripped firmly, walked to the edge and looked down. In his face, dimly revealed in the fitful moonlight, there was no pity but a look of baffled vengeance. Down at the foot of the bluff the shadows lay deep and hid all they held, but out in the trail something moved, rose up and stood still a moment, his face turned upward to where stood Weary.

"Are yuh hurt, Irish?" Weary called anxiously down to him.

"Never touched me," came the answer from below. "He got my horse, damn him! and I just laid still and kept cases on what he'd do next. Come on down!"

Weary was already climbing recklessly down to where the shadows reached long arms up to him. It was not safe, in that uncertain light, but Weary was used to taking chances. Irish, standing still beside the dead horse, watched and listened to the rattle of small stones slithering down, and the clink of spur chains upon the rocks.

Together the two went into the shadows and stood over a heap of something that had been a man.

"I never did kill a man," Weary remarked, touching the heap lightly with his foot. "But I sure would have, that time, if he hadn't dropped just before I cut loose on him."

Irish turned and looked at him. Standing so, one would have puzzled long to know them apart. "You've done a lot for me, Weary, this trip," he said gravely. "I'm sure obliged."

***END

Made in the USA
Coppell, TX
14 December 2019